DONKEY ON THE DOORSTEP

Stephen Greenaway delivered his final word. 'Like I said, if the old fool never comes back, so much the better! If he does, I'll get straight on the phone to the market. I'll send him down there right away!'

Mandy's heart sank. The market for a thirty-year-old donkey meant only one thing – the slaughterhouse. Andi rushed towards Dorian as though to save him from this dreadful fate. Mandy gave him one quick hug and fled across the yard. She left him trembling on the Greenaways' doorstep.

'You hear me! That donkey has got to go!' Stephen Greenaway insisted.

LUCY DANIELS

Donkey
—on the—
Doorstep

Illustrations by Shelagh McNicholas

Hodder
Children's
Books

a division of Hodder Headline plc

Special thanks to Jenny Oldfield.
Thanks also to C. J. Hall, B.Vet.Med., M.R.C.V.S. for reviewing
the veterinary information contained in this book.

Text copyright © 1995 Ben M. Baglio
Created by Ben M. Baglio London W6 0HE
Illustrations copyright © 1995 Shelagh McNicholas

First published in Great Britain in 1995
by Hodder Children's Books
This edition published in 1997

A catalogue record for this book is available from the British Library.

ISBN 0 340 71346 1

Typeset by Avon Dataset Ltd, Bidford-on-Avon B50 4JH

Printed and bound in Great Britain by
Clays Ltd, St Ives plc

Hodder Children's Books
a division of Hodder Headline plc
338 Euston Road
London NW1 3BH

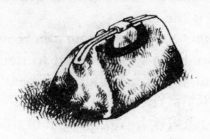

One

The old donkey stuck his hairy brown face over the stable door. He tilted his head to one side as he watched Mr Hope fighting to save the life of the Greenaways' show horse, Ivanhoe.

Mandy had come along to watch her father at work, but the horse had reacted badly to the vet's treatment for nettle-rash. His limbs began to shake, his eyes rolled, and he started to sway. To make it worse, the donkey's worried face continued to stare at them.

Mandy's mouth went dry and her heart thumped. She knew her dad was a good vet; one of the best; but now his skill was being tested to the limit. Ivanhoe crashed to the ground and his legs pedalled the air.

Are you sure you know what you're doing? the donkey's stubborn face seemed to demand. He stood on the doorstep shaking his head.

'Get out of the light, Dorian!' Stephen Greenaway backed the donkey out of the doorway to give Mr Hope more breathing space. Mandy crouched down beside the horse to cradle his head. Ivanhoe's skin quivered all over in reaction to the vet's antihistamine drug.

'He will get better, won't he?' Mandy whispered.

Her father licked his dry lips. 'I don't know. I've only seen this twice before. We'll have to wait and see.'

Outside in the stable yard, Dorian stamped his feet and brayed.

The beautiful horse lay helpless. Mandy knew it was serious and the end could come any moment. An iron grip seemed to clutch at her throat as she blinked back the tears.

'Steady on, boy. Steady on!' Mr Hope ran his hand up and down the animal's fine neck. 'Don't give up on him yet,' he whispered to Mandy. Then he went over to the anxious owner who stood with his arms crossed.

'Ivanhoe,' she pleaded softly, kneeling over him. He was a lovely thoroughbred, a black and white pinto Arabian. Mandy pictured him out on the moor top, cantering in the wind with Andi Greenaway on his back, and in the lanes down into the village. He was one of the finest horses in this part of Yorkshire, a prize-winner at the Welford Show. And now he lay stretched out in the straw, taking great shuddering breaths. 'Get up, boy. Come on, you can make it!'

She glanced up at the two men framed in the doorway, saw the donkey still trying to poke his nose in from behind. For a moment Mandy wished with all her heart that she wasn't a vet's daughter, that she didn't live at Animal Ark, and that she didn't have to sit by and watch beautiful creatures die like this.

But that moment passed. The horse raised his head, then he eased himself on to his chest. Mandy gasped and sat back on her haunches. 'That's it. Come on, boy. Come on!' She stared as he got shakily to his feet.

'Good lord!' Mr Greenaway looked stunned.

Mandy's dad's face broke into a grin. Mandy jumped up. Stephen Greenaway heaved a sigh of relief and shook Mr Hope by the hand. As Ivanhoe stood and pawed the cobbled floor, his iron horse-shoe struck a spark. He'd recovered as suddenly as he'd collapsed.

Dorian butted and barged his way back into the stable. He came up to Ivanhoe to check him over. A bit shaky, a bit dazed; and no wonder! The donkey nuzzled up to the Arabian's head. *Trust them and their newfangled medicines*, he seemed to say. *All that was wrong in the first place was a touch of nettle-rash!*

Mandy gave a delighted laugh. She heard her father explain to Mr Greenaway. 'Ivanhoe must have suffered an unusually severe reaction to the medicine,' he said. 'One chance in ten thousand. But he's a fine, strong horse with plenty of will power, and that's seen him through. I wouldn't be surprised if having the old donkey fussing about in the background didn't help him as well. They seem pretty good friends, those two.'

'They always have been,' Stephen Greenaway agreed.

Mr Hope scratched his bearded chin and asked if the horse was taking any other medication before they'd called him in. 'I think we may have mixed two drugs without realising. That could have brought about the drastic collapse.'

Mandy heard their voices grow more distant as they walked across the yard towards the house. She wanted to stay with the patient, just in case. She put one arm round Ivanhoe's neck, and one arm round Dorian. The donkey blinked back at her with his huge, almond-shaped eyes. It was easy to imagine what he must be thinking now. *When you've lived as long as I have*, he seemed to say with his wise old expression, *you learn to let nature take its course. Some of these young vets, they don't realise that.*

Mandy laughed at him and scratched his nose. 'Yes, yes, we know,' she murmured. 'You've been around an awful long time, and no one knows better than you do, Dorian. We all admit that!'

Eventually she tore herself away from the two friends. She took her jacket from a hook by the haynet and gave Ivanhoe one last gentle stroke on the muzzle. Dorian, not wanting to be left out, barged in for his share. She scratched his bony head between his ears. When she closed the stable door and looked back, Dorian was pulling himself up to his full twelve hands, standing there and peering out. He flicked his long, pointed ears and bared his teeth in what looked like a smile. His stiff, upright mane was neatly trimmed, his dark muzzle and rubbery lips curled upwards at the corners. He was obviously snickering goodbye.

Mandy crossed the Greenaways' yard in the evening sunlight. It struck her full in the face with its warm orange glow. She had to shield her eyes to make her way to the old stone porchway of Manor Farm.

'In here, Mandy,' her father called from the kitchen.

She joined them in the low-beamed, quaint old room.

'How's Ivanhoe?' Mr Hope asked.

'He's fine. As good as new, and the nettle-rash has gone too.' She'd checked the horse's flanks for the round, flat spots. They had seemed to vanish before her eyes. He was a perfect specimen once again.

'Thank heavens for that,' Stephen Greenaway chipped in. He reached for his car keys in the middle of the solid kitchen table. 'Will there be any after-effects, do you think?'

Mr Hope shook his head. 'Unlikely. You were saying you've got buyers coming in to look at him?'

Mandy held back a gasp of surprise.

Stephen Greenaway was a tall, brisk, fit-looking man with short, dark hair and a tanned face. He nodded. 'Yes. That's why we were so keen to be rid of the rash. We're trying to sell him. Andi's really upset about it, of course. It's a hard decision for us to make, but it has to be done. She knows that if you want something in this life, you have to go for it one hundred per cent. That might involve giving something up too. In this case, the horse.'

Mandy bristled at his tone as he pronounced the word 'horse'. *Ivanhoe has a name,* she wanted to point out. Mr Greenaway talked about selling him as if he was a car.

'Why does Andi have to give him up?' she asked.

Mr Greenaway glanced at his watch. 'She's fourteen now. She has to concentrate on other things.' He looked out of the window up the drive.

'Exams?' Mandy knew school work could sometimes crowd out a pastime like riding.

'No, tennis.'

She stared back at him. How could anyone consider giving up a horse like Ivanhoe just for the sake of a game? Even though Mandy and her best friend, James Hunter, liked to play tennis, she would still always put animals first.

'Here's Andi and her mother now,' he said, giving her a brief smile. 'Why not ask her?'

Mandy heard a car crunch down the long drive.

Manor Farm stood well out of the village, further down the same lane as Animal Ark and Lilac Cottage, her gran and grandad's place. It was tucked away in the valley with two or three acres of land, but it was no longer a farm. The Greenaways had turned it into a lovely, luxurious home, with plenty of room in the grounds for Ivanhoe and Dorian. Mr Greenaway was the manager of a successful premier league football team. He travelled seventy-five kilometres to work and back each day. He was a busy man.

'I'm glad the horse made it all right,' he told Adam Hope. 'Would you tell Silvia she doesn't need to put the buyers off from coming over after all. But ask her not to agree to a price until we've talked it over, OK? She'll take care of your bill, Adam. Thanks very much. Sorry, I must dash.' And he strode out to his gleaming black sports car, with only a brief wave for his wife and daughter.

'Don't frown, Mandy,' Mr Hope warned. 'You'll get wrinkles!'

'Well!' she said. 'Tennis!' She felt too angry to put her feelings into words.

'Andi's a good player; county standard. They think she could even become a professional eventually. To get that good you have to practise for hours every day!' He rummaged in the pocket of his leather jacket for his own car keys. 'Come on, let's go and have a word with Silvia. We've done all we can here.' And he led her out of the kitchen, back into the warm rays of the setting sun.

As soon as Andi caught sight of the Animal Ark Land-rover parked in their yard, she ran to meet them. She clutched a tennis bag in one hand and was wearing her sports gear; a trim blue and white track suit and white tennis shoes. Her long hair, blonder even than Mandy's, was tied back in a high pony-tail. Her face looked worried. 'What's wrong? It's Ivanhoe, isn't it? Is he OK?' She began to dash towards the stable, followed by Mandy, Mr Hope and Mrs Greenaway.

Whoa there, steady on! Dorian, the donkey, stood at the stable door, mouthing and shifting gently from hoof to hoof. He seemed to have everything under control, as usual. He nodded towards Ivanhoe in his quiet, dark stall, then he stepped back to let them enter; but only Andi and Mr Hope. *Not too many visitors, or you'll tire him out,* he seemed to suggest. Mandy and Silvia Greenaway took the hint and waited outside.

Andi checked Ivanhoe and saw her horse standing untroubled and healthy, nibbling at his hay. She took a deep breath and came back out into the yard, squinting in the sun. She flung a relieved arm round Dorian and rested her head against his soft brown neck. 'Thank heavens he's OK. Come on, boy, let's get you out into the paddock.'

The donkey, suddenly docile and meek as a lamb with Andi, nodded and walked on.

'Do you want to come?' Andi invited Mandy.

Mandy checked with her dad. She didn't need a second invitation. Soon she strode alongside Dorian and his mistress. She began firing donkey questions at Andi. 'How often do you groom him? How do you trim his mane? Aren't they supposed to be very stubborn animals?' she said in a rush.

Andi laughed. She opened the paddock gate and followed Dorian into the sloping field full of buttercups and clover. 'Don't let Dorian hear you call him stubborn. He won't like it. "Clever" is OK, though. Donkeys are very intelligent, aren't they, boy?' She let him poke his round face close to her own. 'See, he understands every word I say. And he's brilliant with Ivanhoe. To tell the truth, thoroughbreds can be a bit highly-strung, but

Dorian has a knack of calming him down. Don't you, boy?' She fondled the donkey's chin and sighed. 'He's going to miss him when he goes.'

'What about you?' Mandy asked. 'Aren't you going to miss him too?'

Andi sighed. 'I try not to think about it too much. As for Dorian, it's as if he understands every single thing that goes on around here. Sometimes I think he's even talking to me!' She blushed and smiled at Mandy.

Mandy grinned. 'I know what you mean.' She gazed down the sloping meadow to the stream at the bottom, where hawthorn trees provided shade beside the fresh water. *This must be a brilliant place for a horse and donkey to live*, she thought. 'Do you really have to sell Ivanhoe?' she pleaded. Andi was obviously fond of her animals, in spite of her tennis.

Andi hugged Dorian round his neck and buried her face in his coat. The donkey leaned his cheek against her shoulder. *There, there,* he seemed to say.

'Dad and I agreed. He has to go. He's worth a lot of money, you see. It'll help pay for my tennis coaching.' She sighed and her eyes filled with tears.

Yes, she does love them both, Mandy thought.

Andi looked up. She spoke sadly. 'I don't think we'll get much for you though, Dorian! You're not worth anything!'

Dorian sniffed and tossed his head. It was true; he was an old, ambling, shambling donkey with a hairy face and a girth like a barrel.

'Lord knows what we're going to do with you, though!' Andi sounded as though she would break down completely, then she pulled herself together. They heard Silvia Greenaway and Adam Hope leading Ivanhoe across the yard down towards the paddock.

'Dad's right, as usual. I love Ivanhoe and Dorian to bits, and I'll miss them dreadfully. But I have to concentrate on my tennis if I want to get really good.'

'But why not keep your animals? Why do you have to get rid of them?' Mandy tried hard to see the Greenaways' point of view.

Again Andi sighed. 'Now is the right time. Dad's got a new job and we all have to move down south. The new house doesn't have any grounds to keep animals in.'

Mandy nodded. 'I see.' She still studied the pinto as Mrs Greenaway turned him into the paddock.

He was fifteen hands, head and shoulders above stumpy Dorian. His neck arched gracefully, his face was long and slim, his white mane flowed against his black and white shoulders. He picked up his dainty feet like a dancer poised to pirouette. He was magnificent. *How can Andi bear to lose him?* she wondered.

Once Adam Hope was satisfied with Ivanhoe's full recovery, he passed on Stephen Greenaway's message about the buyers.

Silvia leaned both elbows on the five-barred gate and nodded. She gave her daughter a small, sympathetic pat on the back. 'Such big changes,' she sighed. She spoke softly, with a foreign accent. Mandy knew she came from Finland, and Andi had inherited her blonde hair and pale grey eyes from her. Mandy thought Silvia looked sad and uncertain as she looked out across the field and the valley beyond. 'And Welford is so beautiful, so peaceful.'

As she left with her father, she carried his heavy bag full of medical supplies and instruments and swung it up into the back of the car.

'Hop in, Mandy. We'd better get a move on.' They were running late. They had two more calls to make; one to Bleakfell Hall to reassure Mrs

Ponsonby about Pandora, her poorly Pekinese, and then on to Susan Price's place with an anti-worm injection for Prince, her pony. It was a typical round of evening calls for the busy practice at Animal Ark.

Not so fast! Dorian had decided he liked them after all. The donkey came trotting up the paddock and along the fence, craning his stubby neck and braying loudly. His short black mane stuck up like a Mohican haircut, and he showed them his old, yellow teeth. Mandy laughed. She couldn't resist going over to him one last time. 'What do you think of Ivanhoe now, old fellow? We did a pretty good job in the end, huh?'

He turned down the corners of his mouth and jerked his head.

'Come on, we're the best there is!' She scratched his chin and gave a cheeky grin. He sniggered. She ran and hopped into the Land-rover, leaning out to give Dorian a final wave.

'He's going to be one lonely donkey when Ivanhoe goes,' she said to her dad. 'And then what? When the Greenaways move on, I don't suppose anyone will want him!'

Mr Hope gave her a sideways glance. 'Don't look at me, Mandy! No waifs and strays at Animal Ark.

That's the rule, remember!'

Mandy nodded. It was a rule they had because they were already short of space at home. Mandy had to be content with her pet rabbits and all the animals brought to Animal Ark for treatment. There was no chance of Dorian coming to live with them. They pulled into the driveway and headed up to the road.

A car was signalling to come down the Manor Farm drive. 'This could be the people who want to buy Ivanhoe,' Mr Hope said. He gave way and pulled on to the grass verge to let it pass, then swung back on to the narrow road. 'Pandora will be wondering where on earth we've got to.' He put his foot down and the Land-rover sped off. 'I expect Mrs Ponsonby's nerves will be all on edge by the time we arrive!' He winked at Mandy.

Mandy smiled. She loved being out on the round with her dad, even if it meant coming face to face with fussy Mrs Ponsonby. She turned to see Dorian tilt back his head and bray at the top of his voice as the buyers' car approached. He kicked his heels and galloped out of sight. Though he was past his prime, he could still get a move on.

Soon he was a dark speck vanishing noisily into the shadow of the hawthorn trees.

No, thank you very much! he seemed to say. *I don't like the look of this new lot at all!*

Two

'Well, *I* don't like the look of them!' Mrs Platt and Mrs Ponsonby were deep in conversation on the doorstep of Animal Ark. Mrs Platt's poodle, Antonia, growled at Mrs Ponsonby's Pekinese. It was several days after Pandora's latest false alarm, and the dog looked perfectly well to Mandy. She got off her bike and eased her schoolbag from her shoulders. Mrs Ponsonby waved Pandora's paw in greeting.

'We don't know where they've come from, do we?' Mrs Platt insisted. She lived with Antonia in a tidy bungalow and kept busy by helping Mandy's gran to arrange flowers for the church. But she was no match for bossy Mrs Ponsonby.

'Who, dear, who? Whom don't we like the look of?' Mrs Ponsonby tried to disentangle her stout legs from the lead of Toby, her other dog, a tough and friendly mongrel. Mandy obligingly offered to help. She stooped to straighten out the lead.

'Those traveller people. They've parked or camped or whatever you call it just down the lane from here, past Dorothy's place. In full view of their cottage! Dozens of them in their scruffy van. Poor Dorothy!' Mrs Platt sighed. 'I'm sure *she* doesn't like the look of them any more than I do!'

Mandy freed Toby and frowned as she stood up. 'I don't think Gran minds, Mrs Platt. Anyway, she says they've parked on common ground. Everyone has a right to use it.'

Mrs Ponsonby raised her eyebrows. 'But dozens of them, you say?' She turned to Mrs Platt.

'Four.' Mandy was quite definite. 'Two grown-ups and two children. They're a family.' Gran had told her all about them since their arrival last weekend. 'And two dogs.'

'See! *And* they have long hair!' Mrs Platt said darkly.

'Who, the dogs?' Mrs Ponsonby looked confused.

'No, silly, the parents. *He* wears an earring!'

'Well, that's not a criminal offence, so far as I know,' Mrs Ponsonby pointed out. 'But bringing flea-ridden dogs into Welford is a different matter.'

'I'm sure their dogs are perfectly healthy,' said Mandy, her blood beginning to boil. 'And Gran says the family is very friendly – and harmless.'

'You wouldn't say that if they camped on *your* front doorstep!' Mrs Platt looked put out. She snatched Antonia away as Mandy leaned forward to give her a gentle pat. Then she flounced off.

'Never mind, Mandy dear,' Mrs Ponsonby whispered.

They went into reception together, where Jean Knox, the receptionist, tried to keep order amongst the assorted dogs, cats, rabbits and guinea-pigs. 'There are some people round here with very old-fashioned ideas. You just have to put up with them!' Mrs Ponsonby announced.

Mandy smiled. She'd never looked on Mrs Ponsonby, with her pink and blue flowered hats, as a pioneer of forward thinking in the village. But just then, Simon, their nurse, stuck his head out of the treatment room and spotted her. 'Oh great, you're back,' he said. 'Mandy, I need an extra pair of hands in here. I don't suppose you're free?'

She leapt into action. Reverend Hadcroft's cat, Jemima, was kicking up a bit of a fuss about having her temperature taken. Mandy held her gently on the table. She calmed her down, while Simon continued the examination.

And then it was one busy chore after another until well into the evening. Mandy put on her white coat to assist her mother with the insulin injection for a diabetic fox-terrier. Then she helped to prepare two cats for spaying. She loved the work, and felt it would help her own training as a vet when she finally left school.

So it was late when she and her exhausted parents finally finished supper. Then Mandy remembered the rabbits. 'Can I take them the leftover lettuce?' she asked.

Emily Hope was sitting on the patio with her feet up. It was a beautiful warm evening. The sun on her hair made it look even redder and softer than usual. It had brought out her skin in deep brown freckles. 'Mm-mm,' she murmured, without lifting her head.

Mandy drifted out into the garden at the back of the house, down to the far corner where Flopsy, Mopsy and Cottontail sat and twitched their noses at the smell of the lettuce. They hopped and thumped as Mandy approached.

She changed their water and cleared out the dirty bedding, replacing it with sweet, clean straw. The shadows began to stretch long and deep over the lawn as Mandy went back to the house. She headed for the surgery, to get rid of the rubbish.

'Oh, hello!' she said, startled. She turned the corner to find a visitor. His front hooves were on the doorstep. He seemed to be trying to press the surgery bell with his blunt nose. It was Dorian.

He shook his head impatiently. *I've been hanging*

around here for ages, waiting for someone to show up!

'Dorian, nice of you to drop in!' Mandy said with a grin. 'But do they realise back home that you just popped out for a visit?'

The donkey stood firm on the doorstep.

'Don't you think you ought to let them know? They're bound to wonder where you are.' Mandy rubbed his nose a little sadly.

Dorian lifted his top lip and tilted his head to one side.

'It's late, Dorian,' Mandy said. 'I think I'd better get you back home.'

Dorian blew down his nose. He was in a huff as she took hold of his halter. He backed down from the doorstep, but then he dug in his heels.

Mandy soon gave up trying to lead him off. She didn't want to force him, yet she knew his escape from Manor Farm must be causing concern. 'Dad!' she called out. 'Can you come and give me a hand?'

Adam Hope came running round the side of the house. 'Well, blow me down!' he said. His old-fashioned phrase set them both chuckling. 'If it isn't old Dorian!' He stood in his shirt-sleeves, quite taken aback.

'I told you he liked us in the end!' Mandy laughed. 'After I told him we were the best vets around!'

'That may well be,' Mr Hope mused, 'but how are these best vets going to get the old chap home?'

Dorian stood stock still, legs rigid and caked in dry mud.

Adam Hope looked him up and down. 'Tell you what. You could give him a brush down while I ring Manor Farm and let them know where he is.'

Mr Hope went off for the grooming brushes and soon came back. Mandy set to work, first with the stiff brush to clean the mud from round Dorian's fetlocks. Then she used a softer brush on his mane, neck and chest. 'Might as well get you spruced up while you're here,' she told him.

Dorian agreed. She heard him give a deep sigh as he felt the brush whisk away the hayseeds and dust caught in his long hair.

'Here, try this.' Emily Hope came out into the yard with a hoof-pick. 'If he's been in mud, his hooves will need cleaning out.' She watched as Mandy lifted each foot in turn and picked out the mud and stones from the hoof. 'You know something,' she said with an amused grin. 'I think that old donkey knew just what he was about when he decided to come visiting you, Mandy Hope!'

'Hairdresser and pedicurist at your service!' Mandy chipped in.

'You've got a friend for life there,' Mrs Hope decided. They both turned as Mr Hope came back out of the house.

'No reply from Manor Farm,' he said.

Dorian tossed his head and clicked his tongue. What did they expect?

'I'll walk him back anyway,' Mandy volunteered. 'It's only down the lane. There won't be any traffic. And I can turn him into the paddock if there's no one around.'

They agreed that this was the best idea. Mandy handed Dorian's rope to her dad, then she rushed inside to ring her friend, James Hunter. She had to postpone a game of tennis, arranged for that evening. 'I've got to see a man about a donkey,' she explained quickly. 'Sorry, James. How about tomorrow?'

James sounded resigned. 'A donkey? What are you on about, Mandy?'

'I'll tell you tomorrow. Must dash!' She hung up.

Outside, she found Susan Price sitting in the lane, all shiny and smart in her hard hat, astride an equally well-groomed Prince. 'Hello, Mandy. I didn't know you had a donkey!' she said with a smile. Many pony people were snooty about donkeys, and it annoyed Mandy. She felt Dorian's neck muscles stiffen and heard him sniff.

'He's not ours, worse luck,' Mandy replied. Susan sat upright, with her dark hair pulled neatly back under her black hat, her boots spotless. 'I'm just about to walk him home.'

'I couldn't exactly see you riding the old boy over the jumps at the Welford Show!' Susan grinned down at them both.

Mandy frowned as Susan and Prince cantered away.

'Come on, Dorian, I'm your number one fan,' Mandy coaxed. 'Be a good boy now and take no notice of pony snobs like Susan. They go for looks, not personality. And they don't know the first thing about donkeys!'

Dorian looked down his nose at the disappearing duo. Prince high-stepped his way between the hedgerows with Susan perched elegantly on top. The donkey gave a loud, wicked bray. Then he led off down the drive from Animal Ark, heading down the lane in the opposite direction to Susan and Prince; quite happy to go home now, in his own good time, at his own pace.

'Take care!' Emily and Adam Hope both laughed. 'And don't be late back!'

* * *

Mandy and Dorian headed as one into the setting sun. OK, so he was stout and knock-kneed, with a sway-back. He wouldn't win any prizes. He was hairy and nosy and stubborn, with a will of his own. He'd been everywhere, seen everything. As they strolled past Lilac Cottage, Mandy thought he must be a donkey with a long and fascinating history. She was lost deep in thought when her grandad stood up straight from piling luggage into their camper van. He and Gran were getting ready to set off in a couple of days on one of their touring holidays. He spotted Mandy over the gate.

'A penny for your thoughts!' he called.

Mandy jumped, then waved. 'They're not worth it, Grandad!' She stopped to explain where she was going with Dorian.

'Oh, I just saw the Greenaways' car heading home a few minutes ago,' he told her. 'They should be in by the time you get there. There are big changes afoot at Manor Farm, I hear.'

Mandy nodded. 'Have they managed to sell Ivanhoe, do you know?'

Grandad nodded and pocketed his car keys. He came to the gate for a proper chat. He was looking brown and relaxed in his checked shirt and waistcoat. 'Yep. I saw the horse box drive down there yesterday. Do you reckon that's why this old fellow got itchy feet?'

'Well, wouldn't you?' Mandy pointed out. 'If you suddenly got left all alone?'

'Not likely!' he laughed. 'No, I love a bit of peace and quiet. But your gran is always going on about the Women's Institute and rhubarb jam and what not!' He winked at her.

'Grandad!'

Mandy's gran had come down the path, followed by a complete stranger; a man dressed in jeans with long, dark hair and an earring. 'What's that you say?' She raised her fist in mock anger. 'I can hear you calling me names behind my back, you old rascal!'

Gran came right out into the lane and greeted Mandy with a hug. She patted Dorian's neck. 'Mandy, this is Jude Somers. Jude, this is my favourite granddaughter, Mandy Hope.'

Mandy grinned. 'I'm your *only* granddaughter, Gran!'

'Exactly. My son and his wife had the good sense to adopt Mandy when she was a baby, I'm happy to say. Mandy, Jude lives in the van down the lane. He came to fetch fresh water from our tap.'

'Oh!' Mandy realised this must be the unwelcome traveller that Mrs Platt had complained about. He was skinny and long-limbed, with skin that had begun to burn and wrinkle in the sun. He said hello to Dorian and made a fuss of him. Mandy immediately warmed to him. She said she was walking the same way and they set off up the lane together.

'Welford's a nice little place,' Jude said. He strode alongside Dorian and Mandy. 'We like it round here. There are some friendly people.'

'Like Gran and Grandad?'

'Yes. They're going to let us use their outside tap for our water, even though they're going away themselves. I call that friendly!' He smiled at Mandy.

She grinned back.

'Not everyone's like that, I can tell you,' Jude continued.

'No.' She remembered how Mrs Platt had complained about the travellers.

'Anyway, we'll stick around for a while and look for work; gardening, odd-jobbing, anything. We'll have to see how it goes.'

Mandy nodded, while Dorian nuzzled Jude's pockets.

But they had to split off after a few minutes of easy conversation. Jude's battered old van came into view, parked on a flat piece of grassy land. The site was surrounded by young silver-birch trees and backed by an old drystone wall. The wall marked the limit of Manor Farm land, so Mandy knew they were nearly at their own journey's end.

Two children came running from the step at the back of the red van. They were dressed in T-shirts and shorts of bright, clashing colours and patterns. Their mouse-coloured hair hung over their eyes, and their faces were red as berries from the sun. They ran to Jude and clambered round him, then turned their noisy attention to Dorian. One jumped up at his neck, the other demanded to be lifted straight on to his back.

'Hang on!' Jude put down his water container and tried to look stern. He introduced Mandy to his kids; Skye, who was five, and Jason, three. Still they shouted for a ride on the donkey, and soon got their way. He lifted the pair of them up on to Dorian's broad back, and walked steadily down the lane.

'Good boy, steady!' Mandy encouraged him, as she led from the side. She was amazed by how good-tempered he was with the children, who

squirmed and giggled and slipped about like two peas on a drum. Then they whooped and slithered off his back without warning, running to tell their mum of their adventure.

Their mother was a small, slim woman with short hair dyed a dark maroon. She stood on the grass with two thin, whippet-like dogs sitting to heel. She wore earrings in the shape of dangling silver moons and stars. They caught the light as she picked Jason up. She squatted him on her hip, took Skye by the hand, and gave Mandy and Dorian a friendly wave. Jude nodded goodbye.

Dorian looked at Mandy. He pushed out his

bottom lip to pass judgment. *Nothing wrong with them at all.*

Mandy laughed. 'Come on, boy, let's get you home!' she said.

She was glad to see both Greenaway cars in the yard as she and Dorian finally arrived. The stable door hung open and empty, a reminder that Ivanhoe had moved on to a new home. She decided to go up and knock at the kitchen door to tell them Dorian was back. Then she would offer to lead him into the paddock. But as she crossed the yard, she heard raised voices, so loud and angry that she stopped in her tracks, half-embarrassed, half-afraid.

'Don't bother me about it! And don't make such a fuss!' Stephen Greenaway shouted. 'If you must know, I'm *glad* the stupid donkey has gone missing! At least it saves me the trouble of having to get rid of him!'

Mandy felt Dorian go rigid. Donkeys did this when they were afraid; they didn't bolt like horses, they just stood still. And no wonder Dorian was frightened of Mr Greenaway's angry words.

'What do you mean? We're not going to get rid of him just like that, are we?' Andi's voice rose above her father's. 'You promised we'd find a good home for him!'

Silvia Greenaway's voice, much lower and softer, tried to cut in. 'Stephen, please! This isn't making things any easier! Please try to calm down.'

Mandy hesitated beside Dorian, not knowing what else to do.

'Calm, nothing! She has to come to terms with leaving those animals behind! We've been planning it for long enough, and now it's all gone through. We're leaving Manor Farm, Andi! We've sold up. We've got to be out in a week. Just get it into your head once and for all, and accept what's happening, for heaven's sake!'

There was dead silence. 'I'm trying, Dad. I really am!' Andi began to sob.

Her father's voice softened. 'Listen, this is a good move for all of us, Andi. A better job for me. A chance for you to get the best tennis coaching in the country. This school in London produces world circuit players!'

'But I'm not sure I want to go there any more! Mum, I really don't want to leave Manor Farm. What will happen to Dorian?' Andi sounded as if she was in agony.

'We'll try to find him a good home, like we

said,' Silvia Greenaway promised.

'Who'll want to buy him? No one! He's thirty years old!' Andi wept and wept.

'Maybe, maybe not.' Stephen Greenaway held firm. 'But it's too late to change our minds. The house is sold. Now, come on, Andi, this is a real step up the ladder to success!'

Andi stopped sobbing and sounded suddenly calm. 'Well, I've decided not to go. I'll never pick up another tennis racket for as long as I live!'

'Andi!' Her mother's protest fell on silence. 'Please be sensible. This move is for the best.'

'That's not the point. I won't leave Dorian. I'd rather give up playing tennis!'

Mr Greenaway turned away in exasperation.

'Wait, Stephen. Let her calm down. She'll soon see why we want her to do this. Just wait,' Silvia pleaded.

Mandy edged Dorian across the yard to the kitchen door. She raised her hand to ring the bell. Dorian stood, edgy and restless, at her side.

'I can't wait for her to see sense! We've got a week to get out of this place, that's all! The new people want to move in almost immediately. The whole world can't come to a stop over one ridiculous donkey; you know that!'

Mandy saw Silvia nod and admit he was right. Andi glanced at the doorway and spotted Mandy and Dorian. She gave a gasp.

Stephen Greenaway, standing with his back to the door, delivered his final word. 'Like I said, if the old fool never comes back, so much the better! If he does, I'll get straight on the phone to the market. I'll send him down there right away!'

Mandy's heart sank. The market for a thirty-year-old donkey meant only one thing – the slaughterhouse. She saw Andi rush towards Dorian as though to save him from this dreadful fate. In her own confusion, Mandy gave him one quick hug and fled across the yard. She left him trembling on the Greenaways' doorstep.

'You hear me! That donkey has to go!' Stephen Greenaway insisted.

Mandy ran off up the drive, the dreadful words drumming in her ears.

Three

There was no life in Mandy's game as she played tennis against James next day. Her forehands flopped into the net, her lobs fell short. Today she couldn't care less whether she won or lost.

'Forty-fifteen!' James yelled. He gathered balls from the back of the court and began to imitate a commentator's voice as he stood to serve. 'And it's James Hunter serving for the match! Will his one hundred and twenty miles per hour cannonball delivery outclass his off-form opponent?' His voice was low and urgent. He threw the ball up and served. Across the net, Mandy swung at it and missed.

'Game, set and match!' James leapt into the air. His brown hair fell over his eyes as he landed. He took off his glasses and wiped his forehead, then set them back firmly on his nose. He trotted over to join Mandy on the bench at the side of the court. 'Bad luck,' he told her. He was grinning away at his victory.

'Well done. Sorry it wasn't much of a contest.' Mandy hadn't lost the match on purpose. Her mind was still on the scene at Manor Farm. Andi obviously hadn't stuck to her threat to give up tennis and stay with Dorian. There she was, dashing about on a distant court, in the middle of a serious training session with her coach. She hit the ball with perfect style and timing. It shot low over the net. She was a really excellent player, Mandy had to admit. 'I was finding it hard to concentrate,' she confessed to James.

'Excuses!' James laughed. Then he grew more serious. He backtracked over what might be upsetting Mandy. 'This couldn't have anything to do with the donkey you had to see a man about yesterday, could it, by any chance?'

She sighed. 'Right first time.' James knew her very well. She explained everything; how Stephen Greenaway had forced Andi into selling her beautiful thoroughbred horse, and was now set on getting rid of poor Dorian. She spread her hands, palms upwards. 'It's not that I'm against tennis. I just don't see how anyone can think it's more important than looking after an animal, that's all. Especially if that animal's been part of the family for years and years!'

She turned sideways to involve her grandad. He'd come down to the tennis-courts to trim the grass around the pavilion before he went away on holiday. He was in his summer hat, a straw trilby with a smart black band, and a blue, open-necked shirt. 'I'm telling James about Dorian,' she explained. 'Have you seen him today?'

'No, but I heard him.' Grandad strolled across, garden shears in hand. The air smelt of cut grass. 'He was kicking up a fuss as usual. Why?'

'I'm worried about him, that's all.'

Mandy and James picked up their rackets and headed for the gate with Grandad. They came out into the lawned area by the green and white pavilion.

'I know what you're thinking!' James declared. He flung down his racket and leaned against the veranda which ran the length of the pavilion. 'You think you should have stayed to save that donkey. Just like that!'

She had to admit it was true. 'I don't think I should have just left him there.' She remembered Dorian's sad, forlorn face as Stephen Greenaway had pronounced the death sentence.

'Mandy, dear, he's not *your* donkey,' Grandad reminded her. 'You couldn't just whisk him away without asking.' He settled down into a canvas chair on the veranda, legs outstretched, arms folded.

'I know. But Andi said she wouldn't play tennis ever again if they went ahead and got rid of Dorian. But look at her now!'

For a couple of minutes they watched Andi's athletic smashes. Her face was grim and determined as she struck the ball.

'People say lots of things in the heat of the moment,' Grandad sighed. 'Mind you, it would be a shame if the old chap ended up as dog-meat.'

'*Grandad!*' Mandy was shocked.

'Sorry, love. Not very tactful, eh? I didn't mean to upset you.'

James jumped in to swing the conversation round. 'How long have they had Dorian down at Manor Farm, Mr Hope?'

It set the old man off down memory lane. 'Ten years or more. I can remember seeing that young lady over there perched on his back, a little blonde scrap of a thing, and she couldn't have been more than three or four at the time. Before that, he served on the Golden Mile in Blackpool, I believe.'

'The Golden Mile?' Mandy loved to hear her grandad talk.

'The beach. Dorian was a beach donkey before he retired, so I hear. Up and down those sands, come rain or shine. They wore little brass name tags round their necks, I remember, and their bridles jingled all day long. When the donkeys packed up to go home for a well-earned rest, all the kids trailed after them with their buckets and spades. Next day there they'd be again, queuing up with their sixpences for a ride on the donkeys.'

Grandad was lost in the past. 'Well, eventually Dorian got pensioned off. If I've got it right, Silvia Greenaway found him at a donkey stud somewhere on the coast, miles away from here. She brought him back for Andi, and he's been at Manor Farm ever since.'

'Until now,' James concluded sadly.

'Yes, now everything's changing.' Mandy imagined crowds of children in bright swimsuits riding up and down the beach on Dorian's broad back. No wonder it dipped now, and his old knees turned in with the strain. She was glad he'd had almost a dozen peaceful years here in Welford. But it made it all the more cruel to turn him out now, in his last days.

'The trouble is, donkeys live too long,' her grandad said. He got up from his chair and pulled down the brim of his hat to shade his eyes. 'Children grow up and grow out of their faithful old friends.' He sauntered off to attack a weed that had dared to force its way up through the tennis-court netting.

'I would *never* grow out of Dorian!' Mandy said, half-cross, half-sad.

'No, but you're different,' James replied.

They watched Andi whack the ball over the net. 'Good shot!' her coach called.

When Mandy finally cycled home to Animal Ark, she had only one picture in her mind. It was a picture of Dorian's face; drooping, sad-eyed, abandoned.

'Hello, Mandy love, it's Gran!' The cheery voice spoke down the phone early next day. It was a Saturday, just one hour before they were due to set off on their holiday. 'We've got an emergency here at Lilac Cottage,' she said. 'Well, your grandad calls it an emergency. He's out in the garden trying to get a donkey off his vegetable patch. He says you'll know what to do!'

'I'll be right there, Gran!' Mandy's heart lurched as she rang off. Dorian again! She hoped it was just a friendly visit, nothing worse. By this time she'd begun to imagine gangs of men hustling Dorian up a ramp into a smelly horse box. She pictured their struggle to cart him off to market. Perhaps Dorian had seen them and bolted? She rushed down the lane on her bike to her grandparents' house. Grandad was face to face with a muddy, messy donkey standing four-square in his spinach bed. Both looked as though they'd been pulled through a hedge backwards. Grandad's white hair stood on end, as he hung on to Dorian's halter. Dorian had dug all four hooves into the rich soil.

'Can you do something, dear?' Gran wiped her hands on her flowered apron. Donkey and man stared each other out in a battle of wills.

'Yes, but Grandad will never get Dorian to go like that, not by pulling him from the front in a tug of war.' Quickly and carefully Mandy stepped

between the rows of peas and beans into the middle of the spinach bed. She came up alongside Dorian's left shoulder. 'Let go, Grandad!' she said softly. She took the donkey's halter close to his mouth. Then she pushed him with a stiff wrist and said, 'Walk – walk – walk!' in a rapid, firm voice.

Years of routine on Blackpool beach made Dorian obey. He stepped confidently over Grandad's beautifully tended spinach without damaging a single leaf.

Gran clapped and cheered. Grandad stood scratching his head and shaking it. 'Well, I'll be!' he stammered.

'You'll be what, Grandad?' Mandy couldn't hide a giggle. Dorian was easy to manage if you knew how.

'Never you mind!' Gran stepped in smartly. 'Say thank you to your granddaughter, Tom, before she takes this cantankerous old chap home for us.'

Grandad came round at last from his ordeal. 'Who are you calling cantankerous?' he teased.

'Not you; Dorian!' Gran winked at Mandy. She saw that her face had dropped into a frown. 'What's wrong, love?'

'Gran, do I have to take Dorian back?' she pleaded. She'd come to the donkey's rescue once more. Surely she wasn't just meant to take him back home so they could sell him to the highest bidder? Dorian seemed to agree. He nodded his head wisely and nuzzled close to Mandy's side.

'Yes, you do.' Grandad stepped in to overrule Gran, who'd begun to soften. 'He's obviously escaped again, through the stream and up the muddy bank opposite, by the look of him. Now it's time to go home. The game's up, old chap.' He patted Dorian's neck to show there were no hard feelings.

Gran sighed. 'Uh-oh, don't tell me. It looks like you got too fond of someone again!' She hugged

Mandy round the shoulders. 'Your grandad will tell me the full story, but now you'd better take Dorian back. And give me a hug and say goodbye. You won't see us for over a week, you know.'

Mandy hugged her grandparents goodbye. 'Have a good holiday. Come on, Dorian,' she said reluctantly. 'Walk on. Good boy.' They set off down the lane under a grey, overcast sky. Dorian walked sulkily beside her. She swung a hazel switch behind her back and tapped him on the rump when she felt him begin to drag his feet.

Dorian's face was sullen and blank. He stared straight ahead. For once in his life, he didn't want to go home.

He insisted on stopping by the common for a word with the Somers family. Mandy gave each of the children a quick ride on Dorian's back. This time it was the mother who was in charge. There was no sign of Jude.

'Hi, my name's Rowan,' she introduced herself. 'Jude's gone for a scout around,' she told Mandy. 'We've heard they might try to move us on soon.' She didn't sound upset or worried. Instead, she held out her arms for Skye, who wanted to fling herself from Dorian's back, free-fall. They laughed as she landed safely.

'Oh, they can't do that! You're not doing any harm.'

Rowan smiled. 'That doesn't seem to be the point.' Her earrings hung prettily against her dark skin. Her teeth were white and even.

'But you'll be homeless!' *Like Dorian*, Mandy thought.

'Oh no, we're never homeless.' Rowan bent to pick up her little boy and pointed to the van. 'We're like tortoises, aren't we, Jason? We always carry our home with us!' She reached into a plastic washing-up bowl sitting on the metal step and fished out a bruised apple for Dorian. 'Thanks for the rides,' she told him.

He bowed his head gallantly and walked on.

Perhaps he'd spied Silvia Greenaway walking up the lane to fetch him, because he put on a burst of speed and trotted willingly to her.

'Oh, Dorian, you bad boy!' she scolded him in her gentle voice. She turned to Mandy. 'Thanks for bringing him back. Dorian probably went looking for Andi down at the tennis-courts, didn't you, boy? Poor lad, I think he realises that all good things come to an end,' she added. 'It's amazing what this animal can understand! He's forever watching in at the kitchen door for Andi, and when he sees her go off, there's not a fence or a wall in the whole of Yorkshire that would keep him in.'

Mandy nodded. She handed over Dorian's halter. 'When do you have to move?'

'On Thursday. Dorian has to go on Wednesday, don't you, lad?' Silvia sighed helplessly. 'We'll all miss Welford. But there you are.' Slowly she led Dorian off. 'Even Andi seems to have accepted it.' She turned and waved to Mandy. 'Come on, Dorian, walk on, boy!'

That afternoon Mandy worked alongside Simon in the surgery. First they revived a dazed frog that had been in a collision with Walter Pickard's push-bike. They made sure that the victim was fit to be released back into his pond. Then there were the usual croaky canaries, moulting mice and gasping goldfish. Simon and Mandy helped each one as best they could. Then they heard Mrs Ponsonby's loud voice out in reception and realised that Pandora was to be their next patient; both heaved a weary sigh.

'This I could do without,' Simon admitted.

'Me too,' Mandy agreed.

But Mrs Ponsonby soared in with her snub-nosed

pet. 'She's got the snuffles, my dears! She thinks it's hay fever, don't you, darling? She must be allergic to pollen, poor thing!' Splendid in her pink glasses and turquoise hat, Mrs Ponsonby stood Pandora on the table and awaited their verdict.

Simon looked Pandora straight in the face. The dog rolled her big, dark eyes. 'Now, I'm sure it's nothing serious, Mrs Ponsonby. I'll just give her a quick once-over. It may well be something that will clear up by itself without treatment; probably nothing at all to worry about.'

Soon he was able to confirm this diagnosis. 'Right as rain,' he said.

Mrs Ponsonby scolded Pandora for making such a fuss. 'Tut-tut! You and your imagination, my pet lamb! You're always letting it run away with you!' She scooped the brown furry creature into her arms. 'And I was so afraid she'd picked up a nasty bug from those horrible dogs belonging to those travellers. I didn't want to tell Pandora that, of course. It would worry her far too much! But they were horrible scruffy creatures, with all sorts of dreadful creepy-crawlies teeming all over them, I shouldn't wonder. Poor little Pandora didn't realise the harm she might come to! She's such a friendly girl!'

'Oh, I don't think Pandora could pick up anything from those two fellows,' Simon said. He sounded quite sharp. 'I saw them with Jude Somers outside the Fox and Goose earlier today. They looked in perfectly good nick to me.'

'Jude Somers? You don't mean to tell me that you're on *speaking* terms with those people?' Mrs Ponsonby had changed her tune since she'd spoken to Mrs Platt. Now she seemed dead-set against the travellers.

'I certainly am, Mrs Ponsonby,' Simon said even more curtly.

Mrs Ponsonby drew herself up as she stood by the door. 'I must say, I'm surprised at you, Simon. It's people like that who drag down the tone of this village. Why, one of those dogs actually came up to Pandora and tried to . . . well, you know!'

Mandy felt the corners of her mouth twitch.

'Of course, Pandora made her feelings quite plain.' Mrs Ponsonby continued to hold her nose in the air.

'But I don't see the problem.' Simon seemed determined to have his say, and Mandy admired him for it. Though he was a mild-mannered, studious type with his round glasses and spiky fair hair, he could stand firm if he had to. 'They're parked on common ground, aren't they?'

Mandy decided to back him up. 'They're really very nice, Mrs Ponsonby. And I'm sure their dog was only being friendly!'

Mrs Ponsonby sniffed, and the flowers on her hat trembled. '*Common* ground is the proper place for them!' she retorted. 'For common is what they are, and the sooner they're gone the better!' She and Pandora swept out of the door in a terrible temper.

Mandy looked at Simon. 'Count to ten!' he said.

She took a deep breath instead. But when Mandy cycled down past Gran and Grandad's empty house, after breakfast next morning, she was sad to look down from Lilac Cottage into the dip of the common, and see only a patch of flattened grass; no battered van, no smiling children.

Her spirits sank. The Somers had been forced to move on. And now there seemed little hope for Dorian too. Sunday was creeping towards Monday, and the final deadline for the poor old donkey was approaching.

Four

Dorian had no intention of taking the decision to sell him off to Walton Horse Market lying down; or standing up for that matter. In fact, he'd no intention of getting sent there at all. Before Sunday was over, he'd gone missing again.

'Hello, Welford 703267?' a frail voice asked as Mandy picked up the phone.

'Hello, this is Welford 703267, Animal Ark,' Mandy said breathlessly. She'd rushed in from the garden to answer it. 'Can I help?'

'Oh dear! Oh yes, I certainly hope so. Joan, it's eating the asparagus fern! Oh my!' The female voice fluttered helplessly.

'Miss Marjorie?' Mandy put one hand over the phone and signalled for James to come in from the garden. It looked as though their plan for a quiet stroll down to the tennis-courts would have to be put off. 'Hang on a moment, I think we're going to be needed.' She turned back to the phone. 'Miss Marjorie? Is there anything wrong?'

Marjorie Spry was one of identical twins who lived by themselves in a huge old house on the Walton Road. The Riddings was a dusty, old-fashioned place covered in ivy, and the twins were eccentric old ladies. But they'd given a good, kind home to Patch, a homeless kitten, and Mandy was anxious to help them when she could.

'Oh dear! Now it's eating the yucca! Oh, shoo! Oh dear, Joan, put away that umbrella. You'll frighten the poor thing!'

Mandy could hear the panic in the old lady's voice. She had a sudden flash of realisation and her blood ran cold. 'Miss Marjorie, you don't have a donkey down there by any chance, do you?'

'Oh yes, dear! How clever of you! As a matter of fact we do. That's why I'm telephoning. You see, I have absolutely no idea what to do. I can spy him now through the window. He's got himself into our conservatory, and I must say he has rather a healthy appetite. He's eating all our plants!'

In the background, Mandy heard a crash and a little squeal from the other sister, Joan. Her mouth fell open and her blue eyes widened as she imagined the chaos at The Riddings. 'Hold on, Miss Marjorie; we'll be right over!'

'Oh, yes please, dear! Oh my! Joan, don't do that! Oh, good gracious! Now look here, just a minute!' There was another crash. The phone went dead.

'Come on!' Mandy urged a bewildered James. 'Let's go!'

They ran out, grabbed their bikes and helmets, and cycled up the lane into the village. 'It's Dorian. I don't know exactly what's going on,' Mandy panted. 'But the sooner we get there the better!' They pedalled fast and furious, out along the Walton Road. Soon the pointed towers and ivy-covered walls of the ancient house came into view.

A figure flew down the grand front steps to greet them as they flung down their bikes and ran up the gravel drive. Marjorie Spry was dressed in a bright flowered dress, her wispy grey hair coming loose from its bun, her thin arms waving like windmills. 'Oh, here you are, dears! This way, this way!' She ran with little tottering steps round the side of the big house to the conservatory at the back.

Mandy and James chased after her into the glass extension. Its iron arches soared overhead on beautiful branching pillars. Its glass panes, green with moss and decades of hothouse growth, let in a misty sunlight. The inside was a jungle, thick with shiny tropical leaves and bright orange and pink flowers. For a moment they stood still, hit by the fierce, muggy heat.

'There!' Miss Spry put one hand to her mouth and gasped. She pointed. 'Oh, Joan, do come down and behave yourself,' she said crossly.

Joan Spry was perched like a parrot on a high ledge at the back of the conservatory. She gave little, bird-like jerks of her head, and jabbed at the enemy with fierce pecks of her pointed nose. 'You don't frighten me!' she squawked, though she cowered on the ledge. Brawny Dorian stood nose to nose, a sullen look in his eyes. There was a trail of vine leaves hanging from his mouth.

'Can you do something?' Miss Marjorie pleaded. 'I'm afraid Joan will do the poor creature some damage!'

James hid a smile. He frowned at Mandy. 'Shall we creep up on him from either side?' he

suggested. Dorian hadn't spotted them, so intent was he on bullying the twitchy old lady.

'No, we'd better not surprise him from behind,' Mandy whispered. 'He wouldn't like that.'

Joan Spry flapped a thin hand at him. Dorian didn't even blink. He began to chew contentedly.

Mandy decided on blunt tactics. 'Dorian, come here!' she called out in a severe voice.

The donkey's head froze. *Uh-oh!* His eyes rolled sideways. Down went his head and he shuffled round awkwardly to face the music.

'I should think so too!' Mandy saw him hang his head in shame. She glanced round at the smashed clay flowerpots and tumbled, half-eaten plants. 'I should think you *are* sorry, Dorian. And so you should be!'

Miss Marjorie tripped forward to help her sister down from the ledge. 'Now don't be too hard on him, my dear. He's only doing what comes naturally.'

Miss Joan glowered from her sister to Dorian and back again. She stood safe on firm ground again and began to pick stray cactus spines from her hair. 'I'll give him what comes naturally!' she threatened.

'Now, Joan, don't make a fuss. We like animals

here. We like kittens! We like donkeys, remember!' She came up to Dorian who'd sidled obediently up to Mandy. 'Take no notice. My sister likes you really,' she explained.

'No, I don't!' Joan snapped.

'Yes, you do!'

Mandy heard them launch into one of their famous rows. 'Let's help clear up,' she suggested hastily to James. She began to scoop earth back into flowerpots and stand them upright, glad to see Patch, the twins' cat, sitting quietly in an old cane chair in a far corner of the conservatory. He let the argument roll over him, lying in the sun on a faded cushion. He was obviously used to it.

'Will Geoffrey be able to rescue the plants?' Mandy asked. Their old gardener worked long hours to keep the place in good order. She propped some broken stems against their canes, and waited for the twins to run out of steam.

' . . . I don't!'

'You do! Anyway, he's a lovely old thing! I could have a better conversation with that donkey than I could with you any time!' Miss Marjorie said, crushing her sister Joan with a final burst of spite. She turned to Mandy. 'Geoffrey's no longer with us,' she told her.

'Oh, I'm sorry . . .' For a moment Mandy was lost for words. The crabby old gardener was part of the furniture at The Riddings, in his baggy old corduroys and flat cap.

'No, no, he's not dead. He's retired and gone to live with his sister in York.' Miss Marjorie's glance alighted on James. 'You don't happen to know of an odd-jobbing gardener, do you?' It seemed from the glint in her eye that she thought James was the very thing; sturdy, young and agile. She'd have him clipping the lawns before he could say Jack Robinson.

'Don't be silly, he has to go to school!' Miss Joan crowed.

'Oh!' Miss Marjorie looked crestfallen.

'Even in *your* day, boys still went to school until they were fourteen, you know!' Joan was triumphant.

Mandy began to lead Dorian out on to the terrace. She was glad to be in the fresh air again – the Spry twins weren't always as shy and helpless as they seemed!

'Oh well.' Miss Marjorie glanced at James as though she hadn't quite given up hope. The twins stood side by side, watching Dorian go, gentle as a kitten. Their flowered dresses were a riot of colour out on the stone terrace. They watched wistfully, hands clasped, feet spread like wading birds, as their uninvited four-footed guest departed. 'If you do hear of anyone who would like a gardening job . . .' Marjorie Spry called, but Dorian had had enough and was already plodding down the drive with Mandy and James in tow. He rolled his big tongue round his teeth and looked back doubtfully at the scatty old ladies.

Mandy paused, while James picked up their bikes at the gate. 'You know, I'm sure Dorian realises what's in store for him!' She thought gloomily of him penned in amongst the broken-winded horses and all the other miserable, old creatures that nobody wanted. They walked in silence towards the village, minds working overtime on solutions to Dorian's problem.

But finding a home for an aged donkey was not as easy as finding homes for adorable young kittens. You couldn't hang a 'For Sale' sign round his neck and leave Dorian in the carpark outside the Fox and Goose, as if he was a used car. Everyone in the village had a friendly word for Dorian as he ambled through with Mandy and James, but no one could give him a home.

Mandy stopped outside the pub. 'Hi,' she said to Ernie Bell and Walter Pickard, two old men who sat outside the door. Across the yard, Walter's cat, Tom, lay sprawled along the wall top, while young Tiddles, Ernie's cat, chased butterflies in the garden. Ernie and Walter both loved animals. Even now, Ernie sat with his pet squirrel, Sammy, perched on his shoulder.

Walter grinned and let Dorian investigate his pint of beer. Sammy peered at the donkey's huge face and darted on to Ernie's other shoulder, out of danger. 'You two look a bit down-in-the-mouth,' Walter observed. 'What's up? Not sunny enough for you?' It was his joke about the lovely weather.

Mandy sighed. She was too upset to explain Dorian's problem to Walter. He lived in a tiny house across the pub yard, in the same row as Ernie. Neither had any space for a donkey.

'Did you know donkeys lived in the desert? It's their natural habitat.' Walter came out with this scrap of information. 'I expect they like this heat.'

'Well, I never!' Ernie shook his head and took a long swallow from his glass. 'So where are you off to with this old chap?'

'Home,' Mandy said in a hollow voice.

Walter and Ernie turned curiously to James for an explanation.

'Not for much longer. He belongs to the Greenaways at Manor Farm. They're moving, so they have to get rid of him.'

'That's a shame,' Walter said, scratching Dorian's nose, but the two old men were more interested in Stephen Greenaway. They launched into a discussion about the merits of his new football team. Dorian poked his nose through the pub door and made a friendly nuisance of himself.

'Greenaway's a good manager. He's tough all right,' Walter said. 'They say he's one of the hardest men in soccer.'

Mandy overheard. 'You can say that again. He's not even trying to find a decent place for Dorian. The man's got no heart!'

'Uh-oh!' Ernie winked at Walter. 'Why do I feel another favour coming on?'

Mandy smiled. Ernie was a retired carpenter who'd often helped them in the past. He would be grumpy at first, but really he was kindness itself. 'I would ask you if I thought it possible, Ernie, but even you couldn't build a stable and put it in your tiny back yard!'

'Ah, no,' he admitted. 'Sammy here might object

to that.' The squirrel scuttled down his arm into his lap and clung to Ernie's waistcoat.

'Looks like you're stuck,' Walter said. 'Unless, of course . . .' He leaned sideways to squint down the main street. Mandy heard the smart click of horseshoes on the tarmac road. Mandy followed his gaze and recognised Susan and Prince, heading towards them. 'I bet those Collinses would have room for one small donkey on that ranch they call a home!' Walter decided.

'If only!' Mandy said wistfully. She expected Susan to ride straight by.

But Susan was in the mood for a chat. She pulled Prince up and smoothly dismounted. Then she led him across. 'Still taking in waifs and strays, I see,' she said to Mandy. She gave Dorian's chin a friendly scratch. 'I was talking to Andi Greenaway about him this morning. She seemed really upset about having to let him go.'

Dorian thrust his nose at the pretty, horsey newcomer.

'Steady on!' Susan laughed, almost over-balancing backwards. 'Prince here will be getting jealous!'

'Er, Susan!' Mandy suddenly grabbed Dorian's halter and beckoned her towards a private corner of the carpark. 'I don't suppose . . . ?'

'No, I'm sorry, Mandy, I honestly couldn't!' Susan said, shaking her head. 'I'd love to take him in, I really would. But my mum would have ten thousand fits. She says Jim has much too much on his plate as it is, looking after Prince as well as the garden. It just wouldn't be fair to ask him to take on anything else!'

Mandy could see Susan's mind was made up. She knew there was no point in pleading.

James had joined them and stood stroking Dorian's neck. Dorian lifted his head and tutted. 'Well, it was worth a try,' James suggested.

'I'm sorry, Mandy.' Susan had the last word.

'OK, then!' Mandy's mouth set in a determined line. A sudden, desperate idea had just formed in her mind. 'I've got one last plan!' Mandy, James and Susan put their heads together. 'Overnight,' Mandy muttered. 'If Dorian could stay at your place for just one night . . . I'd tell him to stay quiet . . . no one need know! Please, Susan!'

Susan narrowed her eyes and bit her bottom lip. 'OK, Mandy. But if my mum and dad find out, I'm in deep trouble!'

'They won't!' Mandy promised.

Then James spoke out. 'Mandy, are you sure it's

worth the risk?' He looked worried.

Mandy glanced at Dorian's wide, trusting eyes. 'Yes, it's worth it!' she said. 'Come on, let's go!'

The Beeches was Susan's splendid, ranch-style home. Susan split off from the others at the gate and rode alone up the front drive. Mandy and James turned and led Dorian down a path that ran along one side of the garden. It was overgrown with hawthorn bushes, and daisies grew underfoot. They'd arranged to meet up with Susan in the stable block at the back.

'Shh!' Mandy warned Dorian. He'd spotted the luxury stables and was bursting to look them over. 'We have to wait here!'

James gritted his teeth. 'What if he starts kicking up a fuss in the middle of the night?'

'He won't. Will you, Dorian?'

The donkey blew out his cheeks and shook his head.

At last, Susan, still in her riding gear, crept out to the back gate to let them in. 'It's OK, there's no one around,' she told them. 'We should be able to make it without being seen.'

They tiptoed across the stable yard. When he reached his new, five-star quarters, Dorian didn't even hesitate. Straight in through the door; best quality hay, a bucket of oats, a handful of carrots. Bliss!

'Be a good boy!' Mandy whispered. 'If you're spotted, don't worry. Susan will say she's arranging for the horse box to take you home tomorrow morning. But it's better if no one sees you!' She rubbed Dorian's nose and spoke gently. 'So don't go arguing with Prince here and making a noise. I'll come and fetch you early tomorrow, OK?'

Dorian sniffed the air as Prince shifted in the stall next door. He snickered quietly, then munched his hay.

Mandy glanced behind at James and Susan. They still looked worried.

'Do you think we're doing the right thing?' James whispered.

Mandy turned to them. 'I don't like this either,' she confessed. 'But which is the worst thing? Keeping Dorian hidden here while I work out a safe place for him to go? Or sending him straight off to the horse market?'

James and Susan both nodded. There was no arguing with that.

'So we'll keep him here for one night. I'll come early tomorrow morning, and I'll set off with him before anyone's up. I just have to make one phone call tonight.'

'Who are you going to call?' Susan leant forward. The secret plan made her feel tense and excited.

Mandy was thinking ahead. She still had one arm round Dorian's neck. 'First, I have to find the name of that donkey stud, the home for donkeys where Dorian came from in the first place. Then I'll have to ring them up. I'm sure they'll take him back once I explain what's happening.'

James and Susan nodded. 'And you'll trek over there with him?' James asked. 'How far do you think it will be?'

'It's near the west coast somewhere, according to Grandad. Dorian and I can do that in two days if I plan the route properly, and take food and everything. I'm sure I can do it!' she insisted.

James nodded slowly. 'If anyone can, you can,' he agreed.

'I'm not so sure.' Susan looked doubtful. 'Why don't we just tell someone? Your mum and dad would know what to do.'

But Mandy shook her head. 'Dad is adamant that we shouldn't take in homeless animals,' she recalled. 'No, this is something I have to work out by myself!' She pictured stealing away before dawn on an early morning trek out of Welford, up on to the moor as the sun lit the sky. 'Don't tell anyone! Promise!'

They promised. 'Oh, Mandy, I only hope this works!' Susan whispered. Her eyes gleamed in the dull light.

'Me too!' Mandy cried. 'But what else can we do? It has to work!'

Five

Mrs Hope looked oddly at Mandy. 'You haven't finished your tea!' She pushed a bowl of strawberries and cream across the table towards her.

'Pass them this way if you're not hungry!' Her dad looked longingly at the bowl. His own was already empty.

Mandy gave him a little smile. She was wondering how soon she could put her plan into action. First of all, she needed to find the address of the donkey stud from a book on the surgery shelf. Then she would plan her journey there with Dorian.

'What's on your mind, Mandy?' Mum asked, her suspicions aroused.

For a moment, Mandy considered again whether she should let her mum and dad in on the plan to save the donkey. But she knew what they would say; that it was a good idea, well meant, but that she'd no right to take Dorian from his rightful owners. *No*, she decided once and for all. 'Nothing.' She sat in their homely kitchen, at a table piled high with homemade bread and cakes. Her spoon was poised in mid-air.

'Fresh strawberries from the garden,' Dad tempted her.

Mandy dipped her spoon into the bowl. 'Sorry, Dad.' Perhaps she'd better eat up after all. This could be her last proper meal for some time. She only hoped that Dorian would have the sense to stock up on the best quality hay on offer at The Beeches.

She ate her strawberries slowly. She must try to act normally. She mustn't go to bed too early, though she had to be up before dawn; she mustn't let them overhear the phone call, she must pretend that nothing was different.

There was a loud knock at the door.

'I'll go!' Mandy jumped off her chair and rushed to answer it.

'What's got into her today?' she heard Mum ask. 'She's a bag of nerves.'

'She's up to something . . .'

Mandy could hear them discussing her as she shot to the front door.

She opened it. Susan Price grabbed her by the wrist and pulled her over the step. Her dark hair hung loose out of its pony-tail. She was dressed in a white T-shirt and denim shorts. 'Mandy!' she gasped. 'You've got to come quickly!'

'Why? What's wrong?' Mandy's heart sank like lead. 'It's Dorian, isn't it?'

'Good guess!' Susan snapped. 'That stupid donkey! You told him to wait at my place until morning, didn't you? As plain as anything. Well, he didn't. He's gone!'

'Oh, Dorian!'

'Yes, "Oh, Dorian" is absolutely right!' Susan stood with her hands on her hips. 'And I thought you said he was supposed to be clever! Do you know where he's headed for now?' She almost spluttered with annoyance.

'No. Where?'

'Let me explain! I heard this dreadful noise through our back door. My mum dropped her best teacup, she was so surprised. There was Dorian with his head stuck through the door, bellowing at the top of his voice. My mum screamed. Dorian bolted. He charged straight across our front lawn down to the road. I set off after him. He was going at a gallop.' Susan stopped to draw breath.

'Where? Where is he?' Mandy demanded.

'Listen! He was heading down the road. And you know it's a dead end from where we are. There's only one place he can go.'

'Oh no!' Mandy pictured the scene.

'Oh yes! The tennis-courts!' Susan was practically in tears. 'They'll blame me, they'll say it's all my fault. I tried to head him off, but he wouldn't listen to me! So I came straight to tell you, Mandy. Your plan for tomorrow is off. It hasn't worked!'

Mandy's mind worked quick as a flash. No point hiding things from her parents now. She would have to own up later. Right now she needed their help.

'Dad!' she yelled. 'Can you drive us down to the tennis-courts, please? It's important. Dorian's escaped again.' She didn't plan to tell him where from; that would have to wait.

Mr Hope came out, car keys at the ready. 'Come on, hop in, you two.' They all jumped in the

Animal Ark Land-rover. He started up the engine. Emily Hope came to the step to watch them drive off.

'We'll be back as soon as we can!' Mr Hope shouted. He turned to Mandy, sitting in the middle seat. 'Just stay calm. Save the explanations until later.'

Mandy gulped and nodded. Her father was brilliant in an emergency. 'It's not Dorian I'm worried about,' she gasped. 'It's the tennis-courts.'

'And what the players will do to him if they catch him, I expect.' Dad nodded and swung the car expertly round the bends. 'I know that tennis club crowd. Those grass courts are their pride and joy!'

'Dorian's hooves will make an awful mess of them!' Susan giggled in spite of herself.

'Exactly!' Mr Hope's eyebrows shot up into his forehead. 'Hoof-marks all over the place. It doesn't bear thinking about!'

They arrived at the tennis club and leapt out of the car, then stopped dead. To their surprise, everything was calm and peaceful.

'No Dorian?' said Mr Hope. He stood and scratched his head.

The hard smack of tennis balls hitting taut

strings greeted them. Couples dressed all in white chased them across the green courts. Over to the left, to one side of the pavilion, Mandy spied Andi Greenaway involved in a friendly game with her parents and James Hunter.

'He was headed this way, honestly!' Susan protested.

'Well, let's just hope he got diverted,' Mr Hope said.

They watched balls whizz over the nets. Scores were called. Other players sat on the grass and sipped cold drinks. It was a perfect Sunday evening.

Suddenly an ear-splitting noise from the river shattered the calm. Mandy panicked. She ran down the side of the pavilion towards the river. 'Dorian!' she yelled at the top of her voice. 'Stay where you are. Don't move!'

'Ee-aw!' Dorian scrambled up the river-bank. His head appeared. He opened his mouth, showed his yellow teeth and bellowed. 'Ee-aw! Ee-aw!'

Andi stood on court, glued to the spot. Stephen Greenaway flung down his racket. He clutched at the wire-netting fence which separated him from the donkey. James quickly ran out to join Mandy round the back.

Dorian had mounted the bank, covered in mud.

Happy to see Andi, he began to trot towards the courts.

'Someone stop that thing! He's going to charge the fence!' an elderly club member shouted. 'Don't let it near the courts!'

A swarm of players made for the scene. They stood shoulder to shoulder, a human barrier.

'That's it. Go forward. Drive it back! Don't let it set foot on the court!' The old man marshalled his troops. His white hair blew in the breeze as he strode to the front line.

Dorian stopped short. He was cut off from Andi by a thin white line of angry tennis players. They

all waved their rackets at him. He decided on a swift change of plan. With a glance at Mandy and James, he veered to one side and trotted off along the river bank.

'Thank heavens!' James heaved a sigh of relief. Adam Hope and Susan had just caught up with them, in time to see Dorian's broad brown rump heading upstream.

'Panic over?' Mandy's dad inquired.

'Not quite.' Mandy pointed back to where Stephen Greenaway had pushed his way to the front of the gang of tennis players. Now he set off in hot pursuit of Dorian. 'We'd still better get to him first, I think.' She ran as fast as she could after the disappearing donkey.

He trotted calmly along the river-bank, past Mrs Ponsonby walking her two dogs in the evening sun. Mandy ran after him, leading James, Susan and her dad. They were followed by the three Greenaways and some of the keener tennis players, all going hell-for-leather. Mrs Ponsonby pressed herself back against the trunk of an oak tree to avoid being trampled. Pandora growled fiercely. Toby leaped to join the chase. But the commotion only encouraged Dorian to break into a gallop and surge ahead.

'Whoa!' Mandy saw a tall, skinny figure step bravely in front of Dorian and begin to wave his arms. She recognised Jude Somers, the traveller, trying to head him off. She was only half-glad as she saw the donkey halt and try to change tack. Jude flung himself round the runaway's neck. Mandy put on a final spurt, desperate to be the first to reach them.

'Jude!' She gasped out her astonishment. 'I thought you'd packed up and gone!' Behind her, the others were catching up.

Jude Somers hung on to Dorian's tufted mane, then lunged for his halter. 'We did. But we didn't go far. There's a small lay-by just upstream from here, well out of the village. We decided to stop there for a bit.' He grinned as he handed the rope to Mandy. 'You don't seem too pleased to see me.' His brown eyes looked bemused by the whole frantic scuffle. Toby bounded by to greet Jude's two dogs. 'Here, boys! Here, Joey! Here, Spider!' Jude whistled them to heel.

Mandy had time to notice their sleek, brindled coats, their graceful pointed faces as they settled quietly beside their master. Joey and Spider. She even grinned back at Jude. But she was too worried to relax for long. 'Why didn't you just stay

put, like you were told, Dorian?' she demanded.
'You were perfectly safe where you were!'

Dorian rolled his eyes. He ducked his head as
his mistress caught up with them. He nuzzled up
close to her, shutting his eyes, sighing deeply.

Andi fell on his neck, nearly sobbing. Soon
everyone crowded round. Stephen Greenaway
seized Dorian's halter from Mandy.

'Oh, please!' Mandy cried out. She felt her dad's
hand on her shoulder.

'Stand to one side,' Mr Greenaway ordered. He
looked over Mandy's head, trying to ignore his
own daughter's sobs. He looked straight at Mr Hope.
'Do you think you can get this idiot thing back up
to Manor Farm in your Land-rover?' he asked.

Dorian stamped his feet and tossed his head.
Mr Greenaway took no notice.

Mandy's dad frowned. 'We have a ramp up into
the back. Yes, I should say we could just about fit
him in.' He sounded calm but cool.

'Fine. Let's go.' He didn't waste words. His face,
red with the effort of the chase, showed that his
mind was made up. As he pulled Dorian round to
face the way they'd come, Mandy leaned forward
to take Andi's hand.

Mr Hope shrugged. 'Thanks for your help,' he

said to Jude. Then he turned to Mandy. 'You can make your own way back home whenever you're ready, OK?'

She nodded. James and Susan were still here to lend a hand with Andi. 'We'll walk back with Andi to Manor Farm, then follow you to Animal Ark.' She felt like crying herself. She never thought the day would end in such disaster.

Sadly they stood and watched a dejected Dorian being led off along the path. His tail swished, his head went down. He was beaten.

Jude Somers looked genuinely upset. 'I seem to have stuck my foot in it; I didn't realise.' He stood, hands in pockets, watching the retreating procession. Joey and Spider lay low, chins at ground level, while Toby bounded all around.

Mandy shook her head. 'You weren't to know. Heaven knows what we were going to do if Dorian had got all the way to the road, in any case.'

Andi sniffed and gradually pulled herself together. 'It's not your fault. It's not anyone's fault. Thanks for trying to help.' She put on a brave face, ready to walk back to the club.

But the day wasn't over. Mrs Ponsonby still had to roll up and have her say. She toiled up the pathway, carrying Pandora. 'Oh, Toby darling!

There you are. Thank heavens!' Her face was pinker than her glasses, pinker even than her hat. She panted up to them. 'What did those nasty doggies do to you, then?' She bent down to catch hold of lively Toby, then stood up and looked down her nose at Jude and his two perfectly well-behaved dogs.

'They didn't do anything to Toby, Mrs Ponsonby,' Mandy began. She heard James and Susan warning her to be quiet. 'They're beautiful dogs!'

'Oh, you're mistaken there, my dear!' Mrs Ponsonby backed off. She eyed Jude with distrust, then she smiled a superior smile. Without another word, she turned and strode away, one dog under each arm.

'Ouch!' Mandy whispered. 'Sorry!'

Jude smiled. 'Don't worry, we're used to it. Some people take against us just because we're travellers. We have to learn not to mind.'

'I think it's a shame!' Mandy protested. She bent down and patted Joey on the head.

'It's because we're different, that's all. People can't cope with us. But we like the life, so we have to put up with some abuse. If it gets too bad, we just move on.' He looked up at the fluffy white clouds. 'It looks as if we'd better get ready to do that again before too long, now they know we're here.'

'Oh no!' Mandy felt it was all her fault. 'Do you have to?'

Jude nodded. 'We're used to that too. We're planning to look for work. Don't worry about us.'

James stepped forward, looking as if he was about to say something. But Jude turned quickly, whistling to the two dogs. They streaked ahead, and he didn't look back to say goodbye. He walked with his long, loping stride, head up. 'Never mind,' James murmured. 'It was just an idea.'

'What?' Mandy only half heard.

'Nothing. It doesn't matter.'

Sadly they all set off downstream. Dorian had already been whisked out of sight, on his last journey home to Manor Farm. They trailed along the green footpath after him, without a glimmer of hope in their hearts.

Six

Things looked serious by the time Mandy finally got back to Animal Ark. She'd confessed her plan to save Dorian to Andi, and now she was weary from the long walk home. Their parting at Mandy's gate had made her feel wretched. Andi's springy stride had slowed to a heavy trudge. She kept her eyes fixed on the ground and had hardly said a word, all the way up from the tennis club.

Mandy stood with one hand on the gate, trying to find something useful to say. But the words stuck in her throat. She could only think of Dorian and how they'd let him down. 'Sorry, Andi,' she whispered at last.

Andi glanced up at her. 'It's not your fault, Mandy. At least you tried. It's more than I did.'

She sounded so flat and hopeless that another lump rose in Mandy's throat. She nodded quickly and half ran up the path into the house.

Inside, everything was unusually quiet. Her dad wasn't humming hymns for choir practice, or pedalling on his exercise bike, or doing any of the usual things he did on an evening off. He sat with Mrs Hope at the kitchen table, obviously waiting for Mandy to arrive. They looked up as she walked in, her lip already trembling, her eyes not quite free of the awkward tears that kept welling up.

'I'm sorry, Mum. Sorry, Dad.' She hovered by the door. 'It was all my fault. I wanted to save Dorian by taking him back to the old stud. But I realise I should never have tried to keep him hidden in the first place.'

Emily Hope gave a faint smile. 'It's a classic case of wanting to help and ending up making things much worse, I'm afraid.'

'Was Mr Greenaway very mad?'

Mr Hope nodded. 'That's putting it mildly. I think I saw steam coming out of his ears.'

'Oh dear.' Mandy slumped into a chair next to the open fireplace.

Her mother came over and crouched beside her. 'You have to understand, Mandy, a man like Stephen Greenaway can't bear to be made to look a fool. Trying to ghost his donkey away from under his very eyes feels that way. I can see his point.' She spoke gently. 'Whatever you think about his treatment of Dorian, your mistake was to try and trick him.'

Mandy took a big gulp. 'I know, Mum. I did it on the spur of the moment. I'm sorry.'

Mrs Hope smiled and gave her a hug. 'Well, next time . . .'

'There won't be a next time!' Mandy pointed out. 'There'll be no more Dorian to worry about after today. Mr Greenaway will see to that!'

Adam Hope got up from his chair and came and leant against the fireplace. He gave Mandy one of his lopsided grins. 'Tell me, how did you plan to get Dorian all the way over to the donkey stud?'

Mandy blushed. 'I was going to head across country, along the bridle-paths.'

'Then he could live out his retirement in peace and quiet?' Mandy nodded.

'Good idea,' her mum agreed. 'Full marks for content, love. Nought for style.'

At last they could all relax and laugh about it. 'You think a donkey stud could be the solution for old Dorian, then?' Her dad pursued the idea as if it was worth considering.

Mandy took a deep breath. She got up and began to walk around the kitchen, almost back to her old self. 'Yes, I do. If he has to leave Manor Farm, it's the best sort of place he could go to. It'd be like an old people's home for donkeys. They'd take good care of him, especially if we got him back to the place he first came from.'

'Did you mention this to Andi?' Mrs Hope asked.

'Yes, but she was too upset to talk about it. I just said goodbye to her in the lane. She's on her way home now.'

'Funnily enough,' Mr Hope cut in, 'the same idea occurred to me as I drove old Dorian back home. I was sure we could do something better for him than sending him off to market. As a matter of fact, I mentioned the Welford Sanctuary to Stephen, just as an idea. I thought Betty Hilder might offer Dorian a welcome there.'

Mandy gasped and ran up to him. 'What did he say?'

'He told me to mind my own business, I'm afraid.'

'Oh!' Mandy stepped back, her hopes crushed.

'But . . .' Her mother clasped her hands together and raised them under her chin. 'Your dad came home and discussed it with me. We thought we might offer to buy Dorian from the Greenaways ourselves. Then we could take him off to this stud, if it seems OK.' She talked slowly, to let it sink in.

Mandy felt she had to sit down. 'I don't believe it!' she said. 'Oh, Mum, that's brilliant!'

'He won't cost much. Practically nothing. We'll give Stephen a fair market price and take Dorian off his hands for him. We feel the same as you, Mandy. The old boy deserves a better end than the one that lies in store for him at the horse market. We both decided that it's something we'd like to do.'

Mandy leapt up into her mother's arms. She was speechless. Then she ran to her father and hugged him too.

'I'll ring the Greenaways first thing in the morning,' he promised. 'And I'll make the offer.'

'Why not tonight?' Mandy wanted to rush to the phone that second.

Mrs Hope laughed. 'No, just let things calm down a bit at Manor Farm. We all need to sleep on it, and Stephen will be feeling better by morning.

Give him a chance to get over the tennis club fiasco!'

'First thing in the morning?' Mandy asked. It seemed a long way off.

'Very first thing,' her mum said. 'Now settle down with a book, or watch some television. Get a good night's sleep. Tomorrow we'll sort everything out, OK?'

Mandy was torn; she felt half-relieved, half-afraid. One more night; then Dorian would be safe.

At nine next morning, Mr Hope picked up the phone to make his offer for Dorian. Mandy hopped from one foot to another as she stood by him in the reception area at Animal Ark.

'Hello, Silvia? It's Adam Hope here,' he began in a breezy voice. 'How are you?'

Mandy noticed his face fall and a frown set in.

'Is something wrong?' he asked.

Mandy stood still. She felt the excitement slipping from her.

'Oh dear, that's very bad news. Yes. Is Stephen there with you? Good. Well listen, just hang on. We'll be right with you. Try not to worry. Yes, OK. I'm sure we can sort this out. Yes, bye.' He put down the phone with a dazed look.

'Dorian's gone missing again,' he said.

Mandy's shoulders sagged. Just when they were on the point of solving everything!

Adam Hope sighed. 'Even worse. Andi's gone with him.'

'They've run away?' She felt herself go pale.

He nodded. 'Apparently. She left a note saying she couldn't bear to let Dorian go. Getting rid of Ivanhoe was bad enough. She said she was sorry but she hoped they understood.'

Mandy was stunned. 'You mean she's given up everything for Dorian's sake after all? Her tennis, everything?' She could hardly believe her ears.

'Yes. She says she's not coming back. She's gone for good.'

Mandy followed her father out of the surgery, leaving her mother and Simon to cope with the appointments. They ran to the Land-rover and made for Manor Farm as fast as they could.

They drew up and ran across the stable yard, into the kitchen, where they met the two haggard faces of Andi Greenaway's parents. A letter lay open on the table in front of them. Silvia Greenaway's trembling hand rested on top of it.

Stephen Greenaway scarcely looked up. His eyes were glazed, his hair out of place. 'We only just found the note, Adam, a few minutes before you rang. I can't believe she would do this.' He shook his head. 'Two days before she was due to move off to a new life, with everything to look forward to. Why would she throw it all away?'

Mr Hope put a hand on Stephen Greenaway's shoulder. 'Look, don't worry. They can't have got that much of a start. Andi's old enough to look after herself without coming to any real harm. We'll soon track them down.'

'Do you think we should ring the police?' Silvia Greenaway asked.

'No, not yet!' her husband suddenly stood up. He ran his fingers through his dishevelled hair. 'Let's go and scout around for ourselves first. Do you have time to lend a hand, Adam?' He seemed desperate to avoid too much fuss.

Mr Hope nodded. 'Of course. But look, once we've cruised round the local roads and if we still haven't managed to track them down, I suggest you involve the police.' He nodded again at Silvia.

'Yes, but not yet. We'd look pretty stupid if she turned up in an hour or two, looking sorry for herself. Kids often do, you know.' Stephen Greenaway was firm.

Mrs Greenaway agreed. 'OK. I'll take my car.

We'll set off in three different directions. That way, surely we should find her soon!'

They all ran for their cars. Mandy followed her father. 'Dad, I'll set off on foot,' she decided. 'I think we need someone to do that; looking for hoof-prints, for a sign to show which direction they took. Is that OK?'

He nodded. 'Good idea. Check in back here as soon as you can.' He jumped back into the Land-rover and sped off up the drive in the dusty wake of the worried parents.

Mandy watched the three cars speed off. Her idea was to go down to Dorian's paddock to check for clues. But first she went to the empty stable and glanced in. No doubt Dorian had been out in the field all night in such mild weather, but she wanted to check something out.

Yes, just as I thought, she said to herself. Andi had taken Ivanhoe's tack from its hook, and a saddle too. She obviously planned to ride Dorian to freedom. Now Mandy knew she must look for heavier, firmer shoe marks; ones that showed he was carrying extra weight on his back. Quickly she ran to the paddock gate, vaulted it, and began her search.

She criss-crossed the sloping field, heading for

the stream at the bottom. For a second, she wished James was there to help, but she was determined to do the best she could.

She expected to find the evidence she needed in the softer ground at the edge of the water. Sure enough, she saw Dorian's oval-shaped prints sunk deep into the mud, heading straight into the shallow water and out the other side. Then they led off up the far bank, turned left, away from the narrow farm road, and across more fields. 'Yes!' Mandy let out a little yelp of triumph. Her hunch had paid off; the trail had begun.

She plunged into the stream and waded through

the cold water, without even stopping to take off her shoes.

Mandy looked carefully for the route which Andi and Dorian must have taken. All the fields were enclosed, with only one gate. So she headed across from gate to gate, careful to stop and check the telltale hoof-prints at each one. She sprinted across the middle sections of the fields, until she finally came to a halt on a road which ran along the valley side, heading up on to the moor top. Which way now? Far off, on a distant peak, Welford's Celtic cross stood out as a landmark. Mandy looked up and down the road, scanning the grass verges for more of Dorian's prints.

In the distance, from the direction of the village, she saw a dark speck on a bike hurtling down the road towards her.

'Mandy, wait!' a voice called. The bike came nearer. It was James yelling at her to stop.

'Thank heavens!' she gasped. 'Am I glad to see you!'

He joined her, breathless and windswept, swooping down the hill into the final dip, heather to one side of the road, green pastures to the other. The breeze blew the grass in silvery waves.

James told her that he'd heard from Simon what

had happened. He'd rushed along to help, and spotted Mandy heading across country.

She explained how she'd found Andi and Dorian's trail. 'But now I'm stuck. The prints fade just here. They must have gone on the road for a bit. But which way?'

James looked all round. 'I reckon they'd go where it's quietest, where there's less chance of being spotted. Up towards the moor?'

She agreed. 'Let's follow the road that way then. We'll have to watch out for more prints cutting off across the moors. OK?'

They set off again. Sooner or later, Andi and Dorian would stop for a rest. James and Mandy could hope to gain some ground, so they watched out for a sighting somewhere on these long sweeps of moorland. They could see for miles; it was a crystal-clear, bright day.

James left his bike at the point where Dorian's tracks began to cut across country again. They tramped for what seemed like several kilometres, with the rough heather pulling at their feet and ankles. They raised bees from yellow gorse flowers, and trampled bilberries underfoot in their rush to cover the ground. Still there was no sign of the runaways.

But up ahead, almost on the crest of the moor, they had to cross another tarmac road, where they came to a large, flat area covered in gravel. This was where car drivers pulled off the road to sit and look at the view. Mandy was all set to wave at the Somers family, whose van was parked there, then to head straight on. There was no time to lose. But James stopped short and ran across to their van.

Rowan Somers jumped down to meet him. The back doors stood open, and when Mandy followed James, she saw little Skye and Jason playing happily inside. They had washing-up liquid and small wire loops which they were blowing through. Their shiny bubbles floated out of the van doors, up into the blue sky. The children laughed and pointed.

'Hi!' Rowan greeted them, friendly as usual. 'You two look hot. Fancy a cold drink?'

James nodded. 'We can't stop long. We're looking for Andi and Dorian.'

Rowan's clear-eyed gaze stared steadily back. It gave nothing away. She handed them mugs full of orange juice.

'I just remembered something I meant to tell Jude earlier.' James gulped the drink. Mandy stood to one side, wondering what he was up to.

'Here's Jude now.' Rowan pointed. He was walking with the dogs up a sunny slope of grass and heather.

Jude waved a greeting. 'Jude, you know you mentioned that you were looking for work?' James reminded him.

'Still am. We're planning to go from farm to farm to see if they need extra hands. We'll find something sooner or later.'

'Well, listen,' James gabbled on. 'I just thought I'd tell you that there's some work back in Welford. It might not be what you're looking for, though.'

'We're not fussy,' Rowan told him. 'We can't afford to be.'

'It's a gardening job,' James explained. 'At a place called The Riddings. With two old ladies.'

Mandy's eyes widened. 'James, hang on a minute. Are you sure?' She couldn't imagine the eccentric Spry twins getting on with Jude and his family.

He shook his head. 'Like I said, it was just an idea.'

'Well, thanks.' Jude seemed surprised and pleased. 'It'd mean cutting back the way we've just come, but it might be worth it. I've done a bit of gardening in my time.'

'Great!' James grinned. He was ready to set off again.

'I hope it works out,' Mandy said. But privately she wasn't too optimistic about Miss Marjorie and Miss Joan hitting it off with the travellers. 'Anyway, you haven't seen Andi and Dorian this morning, have you?'

Rowan folded her arms and looked down at her bright red laced boots. 'Well,' she said doubtfully.

Mandy saw she'd put her on the spot. She would have to explain. 'You probably know that they've run away to try to save Dorian's life. But what Andi doesn't know is that my mum and dad have already worked out a plan to buy him and find a place in a donkey stud for him; a kind of rest home. We're trying to track her down so we can tell her the good news.' It all rushed out in one long sentence. Mandy ended up breathless. She was sure that Rowan and Jude knew more than they were saying.

Rowan blushed. 'Well, I suppose that's different.' She glanced at Jude.

Jude hooked his hair behind one ear and nodded. 'Andi did ask us not to say anything, but we've seen her all right. She says they'll grab Dorian if they find her, and they'll send him off for good. It'd be curtains for the poor old guy.'

He pursed his lips as he considered the problem. 'She seemed pretty uptight about it, so we agreed not to say anything.' He took a deep breath. Mandy crossed her fingers. 'But Rowan's right; this is different. We really trust you two, you know that?'

James and Mandy nodded.

'Well, like I say, we saw her. And you're about to go way off track if you keep going this way.'

'We just lost Dorian's prints.' Mandy pointed back down the road.

'Yes, you've got to go back, turn right, and take that hidden bridle-path there. That's where they were headed about an hour ago.' Jude shaded his eyes with one hand and pointed with the other. 'Andi was planning to reach Moorcliff before dark tonight. That's another thirty kilometres.'

Mandy nodded excitedly. 'Thanks, Jude! Thanks very much!' She was about to rush off when she had second thoughts. 'What time is it, James?'

He checked his watch. 'Five to twelve.'

'Hey, I think we'd better get back to Manor Farm and check in. Dad told me I should.'

James shrugged, uncertain, but Rowan stepped forward. 'Sounds like a good idea. Give them the news about Moorcliff. They can get a full search party out there before evening.' She looked at Jude and he nodded. 'Look, hop in the van with us. We'll drive you back down. It'll be quicker.'

Mandy jumped at the chance. 'Thanks. We can be there in twenty minutes.'

'Come on, then.' Jude piled them into the van. Skye and Jason giggled and cuddled up close. Jude turned in the wide gravel space and revved the engine. The battered old van chugged off along the moor road, back to Welford.

'I hope we're doing the right thing here,' Mandy whispered to James. Part of her wished they'd followed Andi and Dorian on foot. But this was more sensible; they'd let the Greenaways know what was happening and put their minds at rest. She just wished the Somers' van was faster. Its top speed was about thirty kilometres per hour, as it spluttered and coughed its way down the hillside. Meanwhile, Andi and Dorian headed in the other direction, across the wild moor top.

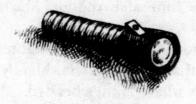

Seven

Mandy and James jumped down from the Somers' van at the Welford crossroads. They stood and watched it chug slowly out on to the Walton Road. Then they quickly ran up the lane to Animal Ark. Mandy spilled out the news to her mother.

'Let's phone Manor Farm right away,' Emily Hope said.

But Mandy put one hand on her mum's arm as she reached for the phone. 'Tell Mr Greenaway where they're heading, and tell him we'd like to buy Dorian from him at the same time!' she pleaded. 'Then we'll know they're both going to be safe, both Andi and Dorian. Please, Mum!'

Mrs Hope nodded. 'OK, Mandy. That's good thinking. I'll get him to agree to sell Dorian to us, so we can see him safely retired!' She dialled the number.

Mandy stood close by with bated breath.

' . . . Yes, that's right, Silvia. Mandy seems to know exactly where Andi's headed.' Mrs Hope's voice stayed calm in all emergencies. 'Look, we've finished surgery here. Why not come over and discuss what to do next? We've a little plan of our own to put to you. Yes, I'll put the coffee on!'

She put the phone down and nodded. 'Well done, you two. This looks a lot more hopeful!' She told them that Mr Hope and the Greenaways had driven round in circles all morning, without seeing a single sign of the runaways.

Mandy went to the bookcase in the lounge to fetch a local map. By the time her father, and Mr and Mrs Greenaway strode up the path, she and James had pinpointed Moorcliff and found the quickest route there. Soon everyone circled round.

'I know that village,' Dad said. 'It's out of our area, but Tony Marsden, the vet there, is a friend of mine. It's tucked away in the middle of nowhere, way off the beaten track.'

Stephen Greenaway nodded. 'I know it. There's

a pub there called The Red Lion.'

Mr Hope nodded. 'A church and a few houses, that's all.' The village sat at the foot of a sheer limestone cliff. Above that, there was a stretch of strange rocks and standing-stones, famous for their wild location. 'The locals call it The Valley of the Giants.'

Silvia looked worried. 'It sounds like a dangerous place.' She turned to Mandy. 'Are you sure Andi is making for Moorcliff?'

Mandy said she believed everything that Jude had told them. 'I thought maybe the best idea would be for everyone to drive up there and form a search party. We can set off from the village. There's plenty of time to get there by car and start looking. Andi won't expect us to arrive there before her.'

'You mean she'll be busy looking over her shoulder, expecting us to follow? So she won't realise what lies ahead,' Mr Hope thought aloud.

Mandy nodded again, then she took her mother to one side while the others studied the map. 'Mum, did you ask Mr Greenaway about buying Dorian?'

'Yes. He agreed!' Emily Hope smiled broadly.

'He promised?'

'Yes. He admits it was tough on Andi to send the old chap off to market. So that's all sorted out.'

Mandy breathed a sigh of relief. In that case, she'd do her level best to help with the search.

'Listen.' Stephen Greenaway went to stand at the Hopes' kitchen window and spoke as he looked steadily out on to the lane. 'I'm grateful for all your help. Especially to Mandy and James here; that was good thinking. But I feel that from now on we ought to crack this problem by ourselves. There's really no need to put yourselves out any more. I'm sure we can manage.' He turned, hands in pockets, smiling confidently.

'Oh, it's no trouble!' Mandy's dad assured him.

Mandy felt worried. The bigger the search party, the better, surely?

'No, look, we really want to help!' her mother put in. 'What are neighbours for? We wouldn't dream of letting you cope with this by yourselves. I know how worried you must both be!'

Silvia Greenaway spoke up. 'Oh thank you, Emily. You're sure you don't mind?' She looked and sounded relieved.

Mandy sighed. What a lot of time they were wasting, being polite. She was impatient to be off.

'Let's go and check again with Jude and Rowan,' James suggested, as the grown-ups finished their coffee. 'We've got time, haven't we?'

'I'll run you down there,' Adam Hope agreed. 'I wouldn't mind checking over what they have to say. After all, as far as we know, they were the last people to see Andi and Dorian.' He'd already arranged his route along the dale to Moorcliff, and now promised to meet up with the others there. 'Come on, you two, let's go!'

Soon they were on the move again, windows open, breeze blowing through the Land-rover, and heading for Welford. 'Where are we going exactly?' Mr Hope asked.

'The Riddings,' James said. 'Jude's gone there to look for work.'

Adam gave a low whistle. 'If you say so!' He pulled off the road and turned into the driveway of the big old house.

Sure enough, there was Jude's red van. Skye and Jason sat cross-legged on Geoffrey's perfect lawn, playing with Patch. Down the side of the house they could hear more voices.

'We don't!'

'We do!'

'Don't!'

'We do, Joan,' Miss Marjorie sighed. The old ladies were standing outside their conservatory, face to face, arms outstretched, like two colourful scarecrows. 'You know perfectly well that we do need a new gardener. We agreed. When Geoffrey left us, we said we'd find somebody else to do his work!'

Jude and Rowan stood nearby, hands behind their backs, looking puzzled and patient. Rowan raised a hand to say hello to Mandy, James and Mr Hope. But still the sisters scrapped on.

'There's a whole family of them!' Miss Joan snapped. 'Even children! And you know I can't stand strangers!'

'But Mrs Somers has offered to do our cleaning, Joan. Though Lord knows why.' Miss Marjorie sighed and glanced through the window at piles of old newspapers and years of dust. 'She seems quite keen to tidy the place up. They will park their van in our big garage and work for us here for as long as they can stand it!' She poked her sharp face even closer to her sister's. 'It'll liven the old place up, so there!' And Miss Marjorie, the boss, turned and shook hands with Jude and Rowan. Miss Joan stormed off.

'Well, I'm glad that's settled!' Marjorie Spry

said. 'Ah, Mandy!' She came over with a delighted smile. 'Let me introduce you to our new gardener, Jude Somers.'

Mandy smiled back. 'We've already met, Miss Marjorie, thanks. It's him we've come to talk to actually. You don't mind, do you?'

Miss Marjorie shook her head and smiled, then went in to sort out her sister.

James grinned broadly at the success of his plan. He gave a thumbs-up sign to Rowan. Meanwhile, Mandy asked Jude if he would mind repeating the story about Andi to her dad. 'We're going to drive up to Moorcliff now,' she told him. 'So we'd be glad if you could remember any other little detail.'

'Anything at all,' Mandy's dad said.

Jude thought carefully, biting his forefinger between a set of even, white teeth. 'Well, like I said, she was riding the old donkey down the bridle-path, heading into the next valley, towards the reservoir at Tindle. She planned to get to Moorcliff before dark.'

'Did she say what she was going to do when she got there?' Mandy asked.

'She said she knew of a place to sleep at a farm over there; a kind of youth hostel. She was hoping to find that, then head on east tomorrow.'

'What time was it when she left you?' asked Mr Hope.

'Around eleven, I think. Look,' he said, as if he had something important to say. 'I feel pretty bad about all this. I could see she was uptight about something. I think maybe I should have tried to talk her out of carrying on.'

'No chance. From what I know of Andi, she's a very determined girl!'

'That's right,' Mandy agreed. 'I don't think anyone could change her mind.'

'OK.' Jude nodded. 'Thanks.'

'No. Thank *you*!' Adam Hope shook his hand.

'We'll let you know how we get on.'

Jude watched them climb back into the Land-rover. 'I hope you find her. I wouldn't like to be out on that moor alone at night!'

His words echoed in Mandy's thoughts. The journey up to Moorcliff was bound to be tense. The road was narrow and twisting, across some of the wildest, emptiest stretches of moorland in all of England.

They arrived at the village green in Moorcliff just after three o'clock. One side of the deep valley already lay in shadow, the other in bright sunshine. Mandy spotted Stephen Greenaway's car waiting for them in the small carpark at The Red Lion. Opposite the pub was a church with a squat grey tower, and beside that a row of low stone cottages, with moss growing on their long, sloping rooves. There was no one on the village green; only a solitary black cat stalking through the grass. Behind them loomed the steep white cliff after which the village was named.

Stephen Greenaway beckoned them across, map in hand. 'Any news?' he yelled.

'First off, we have to look for a farm bunkhouse,' Mr Hope answered. 'Maybe someone should wait there to see if Andi shows up. The problem is, we don't have the name of the farm.'

Mandy scoured the village for signs of life. 'Let me go and ask in that little shop!' she suggested. She ran over the green to the end house in the row of cottages. She'd spotted a sign over the door saying 'Newsagent'. She dived inside and soon emerged. 'It's Bridge Farm Bunkhouse!' she announced. 'Along the riverside, turn right at the stone bridge, then first house on the left, up a long lane.'

The whole group followed her directions, but only the Greenaways went ahead on foot, up the track to the square farm building. Mandy and the others agreed to wait by the bridge, keeping an eye open and deciding how to split up. They wanted to go off looking for Andi and Dorian before evening began to draw in, to make sure they didn't get lost on the way through the bleak Valley of the Giants.

'I reckon we've got two or three hours to search,' Emily Hope said. 'Then we should meet up back here again to reconsider.'

'We'll find her!' James promised. 'She can't just vanish into thin air, can she?'

Soon Stephen and Silvia Greenaway returned.

'Mrs Russell, the farmer, says she'll keep an eye open for Andi. We've told her what to expect.'

'You mean a tired girl and a stubborn old donkey?' Mrs Hope tried to lighten things. 'Not easy to miss, when you think about it.'

'Don't you believe it.' Stephen Greenaway scanned the horizon in every direction. 'When Andi decides to do something, she does it properly. Including disappearing!' He pointed to a hillside strewn with dark rocks. 'That's the bridle-path coming down the moorside from the direction of Welford,' he said. It was already in deep shadow. 'It's the Valley of the Giants. That's where I think we should head for, then fan out and start the search.'

Everyone agreed, and the tramp through the heather began again. They criss-crossed the slope between high rocks. Mandy smelt the peat underfoot and felt the ferns brush against her legs. She screwed up her eyes and gazed around. For miles ahead there was nothing but rocks and moorland, the dark horizon and the eggshell blue sky.

Two hours later, when they finally scrambled to the top and looked down on acre after acre of open countryside, their hopes sank. If a girl on a donkey had been anywhere nearby, anywhere within say fifteen or twenty kilometres, they'd have spotted her by now. 'Not a single hoof-print!' Mandy sighed. She felt exhausted. James sat next to her on a flat rock and shoved a hand through his hair. 'I never thought it would be this hard!' she moaned.

He agreed. 'I guess she changed her mind and went off in another direction.'

'Oh no!' Mandy thought of all the time they'd wasted on the wrong trail. Andi and Dorian could be many kilometres away by now, heading south or north. Who could tell?

Reluctantly everyone agreed they should head back down into the village. 'I'll stay there,' Mr Greenaway volunteered. His face was drawn, his voice quiet. 'I'll stop over at Bridge Farm, just in case Andi finally turns up. You never know, she might have come by a different route.'

'I'll stay with you,' Mr Hope offered.

But Mr Greenaway asked him to take Silvia home. 'There's got to be someone at the house, in case Andi shows up there. One person ought to be enough here.' He squeezed his wife's shoulder. 'Try not to worry too much.'

She took a deep breath. 'If there's no sign of

Andi when I get back home, I'm going to telephone the police.'

He nodded. 'OK, do what you think is best. Here's the farm telephone number. Ring me if there's any news. Now, off you go. I'll scout around here until it finally gets dark. We'll just have to keep our fingers crossed.'

'I've had mine crossed all day!' Mandy whispered to James. There was a pink glow in the sky as the sun settled into the branches of the trees in the churchyard. She thought of Andi trekking with Dorian across the empty spaces, miserable and alone.

No one spoke much as they split off from Stephen Greenaway and drove in the Land-rover out of the sleepy village. By the time they reached Welford, dusk had fallen. Everyone's thoughts were fixed on the lost pair.

Emily Hope asked her husband to stop at Animal Ark. She wanted to drop Mandy and James there. 'Wait inside,' she told them gently. 'We'll drive Silvia down to Manor Farm. Dad will drop me off there and then he'll drive straight back here. OK?'

Mandy nodded. Her mum squeezed her hand.

Then the car was gone, down the lane out of sight. Mandy and James, leg-weary and footsore, trudged up the path and opened the door.

'All for nothing!' James sighed. 'What shall we do now?'

Mandy flopped in a chair by the kitchen table. 'Don't ask me. It looks like it's up to the police from now on!' She gathered her last scrap of energy and took some lettuce leaves from the vegetable rack. 'I'm just going out to feed the rabbits,' she told him. 'It won't take me long.' She walked through the surgery, a short cut into the back garden. The cool air soothed her as she trod across the grass.

'Mandy!' James's voice cut through the still air.

She dropped the bundle of leaves. 'What is it?' She ran back towards the house. James's shout had come from the direction of the front door. She could hear a thumping, rattling, stamping noise. She turned the corner. Dorian!

The donkey kicked at the door. A deep, chesty sound warned them he was getting impatient. He tossed his head as Mandy ran up to him. James flung the door wide open and ran out.

'Andi?' he shouted. 'Where are you?'

There was no reply.

'Here, boy! Steady!' Mandy reached out for his bridle, but he reared up and brayed. His loose saddle slipped sideways, stirrups swinging. 'Oh, Dorian, where's Andi?' Mandy pleaded. 'What are you doing back here all by yourself? I wish you could tell us!'

James tried to reach out and catch the donkey by a length of rope coiled round his saddle, but he too had to back off. Dorian's hooves were up, pawing the air. He charged off down the drive, then turned to look at them.

'Dorian!' Mandy said again.

He trotted up. Again she tried to catch him. He tossed his head, his eyes rolled, he trotted away down the drive.

'James, he's trying to tell us where Andi is!' Mandy gasped. 'Oh, clever boy! Steady! We understand!' She turned to James. 'I think she must be in trouble.'

They stared at the riderless donkey. There could be no other explanation.

'Wait, I'll grab a torch!' Mandy said. 'It'll be dark soon.' She dashed into the house then rushed out again, torch in hand. 'OK, Dorian, lead on!' she told him.

Up went the donkey's head, ready to canter on.

Their legs ached, every muscle groaned at the effort, and night was falling. But Dorian had come to tell them that Andi was in bad trouble. They were the only ones who knew. Grimly, they followed him across fields, heading for the distant Celtic cross, over the moorside towards the Valley of the Giants.

Eight

'Are you OK?' Mandy perched on top of a stone wall and glanced back at James. Dorian stood on the road, snorting impatiently. Half an hour had gone by and they'd reached the top of the moorside. They were exhausted, and dusk had settled in a grey mist.

'Yes, hang on a sec. I've got something in my shoe.' He breathed heavily as he bent forward to see it, but Dorian wasn't going to let them waste any time. Already he had trotted ahead, his mind set on taking them to Andi. Soon he veered off to the right, down the same bridle-path as before.

'Where are we now?' James ran alongide Mandy,

using his arm to shield his face from overhanging hazel bushes.

'We're heading down towards Tindle. See, there's the lake!' Mandy pointed into the valley bottom. The smooth stretch of water gleamed silver under the full moon. 'Dorian seems to know exactly where he's going, no problem.' She ducked under more bushes and took the torch from her back pocket. Its dim yellow light lit the patch of rough grass and heather just below their feet.

'That's better!' James ran grimly on. 'Let's just hope he's got a good sense of direction.'

'Of course he has; look!'

Twenty metres ahead, Dorian stopped. He raised his head and twitched his long ears. The path split three different ways, but he chose the one that led downhill towards the water. Mandy and James followed. Their torchlight bobbed across the rough surface.

Dorian cantered ahead, his heavy hooves startling pheasants. Rabbits darted into their burrows. Dorian ploughed on.

'I reckon Andi must be somewhere down there by the water,' James told her. 'By the look of Dorian's loose saddle, she had a fall.'

'And once she was off, for some reason she couldn't get back up again. Is that what you mean?'

James nodded. 'So he came to fetch us.'

'Whoa! Good boy!' The donkey's flanks were beginning to heave. For a moment the darkness seemed to confuse him. He stopped by a wooden stile and looked all round. Then he caught the gleam of the water once more and headed on. 'Come on!' Mandy said. 'Maybe we're nearly there!'

The lake stretched up the valley; a long, thin ribbon of water. The hillside beyond rose steep and rocky. By now it was pitch black. Sure-footedly Dorian picked his way along the water's edge. He turned his head to keep Mandy and James in view, but he moved swiftly until he came to a narrow wooden bridge over a stream. Here he stood still once more and sniffed the air.

'Listen!' Mandy swung the torch up the rocky slope. 'Did you hear that?'

'No. What?'

'I thought someone called out!'

Dorian nodded and clattered off the bridge, up the slope. He was built to climb these steep, rocky surfaces. He strode with ease from one flat rock to another. Mandy and James found it more difficult. Slowly they heaved themselves upwards, sticking close to the side of the stream, past waterfalls that fell for two or three metres then bounced on to rocks. The water splashed and roared. Mandy used the torch to search for hand and footholds. The climb grew steep and difficult. 'Wait for us, Dorian!' she called.

'I thought I heard something!' James grabbed her arm. 'What was that?'

Another cry travelled down the hillside, faint and muffled. Mandy felt the hairs at the back of her neck prickle. 'Come on,' she urged. 'That must be Andi! She's calling for help.'

Dorian stood just ahead of them, on a rock which jutted over the stream. He was a silhouette against the midnight blue sky as he put back his head and brayed.

Andi must have heard him. 'Is anyone there?' she cried. 'I'm down here! I can't move! Help!'

Mandy's heart thumped, then missed a beat. The voice sounded as if it came from the depths of the earth; somewhere deep down. Now Dorian had found his bearings again. He blundered through the undergrowth until he came to a deep crack in the rock. His hooves clattered to a standstill. He stood perched at the edge of a crevice, about a metre wide, that plunged down into darkness.

'Help!'

'She's down there!' Mandy flicked the torch in the direction of the hole. It was a narrow, sheer drop. Dorian stamped and pawed the ground. 'Andi!' she yelled. 'It's me, Mandy! Can you hear me?'

'Yes!' A voice came back, sobbing with relief. 'Is Dorian there? Is he all right?'

'He's here, and he's fine. What about you?' Mandy sounded calm, but she stared at James in dismay. The torch was too weak to light up the crevice. They could see only the jagged rock-face, small ferns, tree roots and broken branches.

'I'm OK. One arm hurts. I'm cold and wet. There's water dripping down here!' Her voice shook. 'I don't think you'll be able to get me out by yourself.'

'Andi, listen. It's me, James. I'm here too. How far down did you fall?' He lay flat on his stomach and tried to peer down into the darkness. Then he pointed out a pale, blurred shape. Mandy swung the torch. Andi's blonde hair and white face stared back up at them. 'There she is! She's about four metres down on some kind of ledge!'

'Thank heavens you're here!' Andi cried.

James scrambled to his feet. 'She's right. I don't think we can get her out by ourselves. But there's a house along there. Can you see the light?'

Mandy nodded. She steadied Dorian, who pushed at her with his nose. He urged her to do something to help get Andi out.

'I'll run over there to phone an ambulance. You stay here and wait!' James was gone before she had time to think.

It was Mandy's turn to lie down on the ledge, just above Andi's resting place. 'Did you hear that? James has gone for help. It won't be long now!' She shone the torch on Andi. Her fall had been broken by a tree trunk jammed against the rock and wedged there for good. 'You were lucky!' she whispered. She heard her own voice echo. Small pebbles rattled and fell down the crevice.

'You wouldn't say that if you were down here!' Andi said. 'How long have I been here? It seems like ages!'

'OK, don't worry. We'll soon have you out!' But Mandy could see that it was impossible to reach down and pull the injured girl to safety. They would have to wait for James.

'My legs are numb and one arm's useless. Mandy, I don't know how much longer I can hang on!' Andi cried. 'I feel as if I'm slipping off!'

'No! Stay still. I'll think of something!' She leapt to her feet. 'Listen, Andi, you know there's this length of rope round Dorian's saddle? I'm going to see if I can do anything with that.'

'OK, but it's not very long,' Andi warned her. Her voice seemed to fade, as if her strength was failing. 'I brought it for emergencies. Yes, give it a try!'

Mandy took the rope and began to make a loop at one end. It had to be big enough for Andi to slip her head and shoulders through. Setting the torch on the ground, she worked quickly in its shaft of light. Soon the rope was ready. 'Andi, I'm going to hang on to this end and send the noose down to you, OK? You'll have to see if you can grab hold of it and wriggle into it!'

She held the torch now and watched as the rope snaked down into the dark space. 'Please let it be long enough!' she whispered. She craned over the edge, with Dorian close behind her. His breath was hot on her neck.

Andi reached and grabbed the loop. 'Got it!'

'Good! Now wriggle into it, if you can!'

Andi did as she was told. She was awkward and slow because her left arm hung useless. Her face showed the pain she must be feeling. 'Done it!' she gasped at last.

'Well done! Now if you topple off, at least you won't fall all the way to the bottom. I'm here to stop you!' Mandy sounded more confident than she felt. She gazed up at the track where James had run, towards the house by the dam. 'Hurry up!' she begged in a whisper, through clenched teeth. She felt her knuckles tighten over her end of the rope. Would Andi last out? Looking at Dorian, she began to pray.

The donkey seemed to understand. He'd watched the rope being lowered. He'd seen Mandy take the strain at this end. Now he had his own idea. He came close and put his head on Mandy's shoulder, nudging sideways at her face.

'Not now, Dorian. I can't let go!' At first she thought he wanted her to stroke him and tell him what a clever old thing he was. She dug her heels against a ridge in the rock and leant backwards, taking the strain. 'Are you still OK down there?' she yelled.

The answer came back, faint and unsure.

Again Dorian nuzzled Mandy's face. He jerked his neck away, then offered his nose again. His bridle jingled and the red nylon rein swung forward across her shoulder. He stood patiently waiting.

'Oh, I see!' At last Mandy got the idea. She took the rein in one hand. 'Listen, Andi! Dorian's offering to help. He's strong, isn't he? He seems to think he can pull you clear. What do you think?'

'Yes!' Andi gasped. 'Good idea! Do it, Mandy! Do it quick!'

She took the thick rope and threaded it through Dorian's halter ring. She tied it securely. He edged away from the drop, pulling the rope tight. 'Whoa!' Mandy craned forward, one hand on his shoulder. 'Ready, Andi?'

There was no reply. Mandy could see a blurred

shape slumped forward. But Andi was still conscious. She glanced up and nodded weakly.

'OK,' Mandy said softly to the old donkey. 'It's all up to you. When I give the word, pull slowly and gently. Ready?'

Dorian stood steadfast, awaiting the order.

Mandy took one last look down the gap. 'Steady, boy!' She took a deep breath. 'Now walk on!'

Dorian pulled. Pebbles dislodged and dropped with a hollow rattle. The rope strained and creaked. Andi shifted from her wedged tree trunk and hung suspended in mid-air. 'Grab a hand-hold!' Mandy urged. She turned back to Dorian. 'Walk on, boy!' she urged. 'Gently, gently!' Slowly he eased Andi out of the crevice.

At last the fingertips of her right hand could grab the ledge. 'I've got you!' Mandy cried. She felt the sweat start out on her brow. She saw Dorian's sides begin to heave. 'Steady, boy!' she warned. Andi's hand grasped hers. 'OK, Dorian, now one last pull!'

Andi's shoulders appeared at ground level. 'Now use your legs. Find a foothold!' Mandy said. Even with Dorian taking most of the weight, she was in danger of being pulled too close to the edge herself.

'I can't. My legs are numb!' Andi cried out, terrified. But the fresh breeze seemed to revive her. She kicked against the rock-face and found a ledge. Gradually Dorian heaved her up, centimetre by centimetre.

Mandy hooked both arms under Andi's armpits and pulled. 'Walk on, Dorian!' This was it; the final heave.

Dorian responded. Andi came clear. Mandy staggered backwards with her as she found herself on firm ground once more. Then they stood and hugged each other, leaning against Dorian, gasping with relief.

Now they would have to wait in the dark as the light of the torch was beginning to fade. Mandy put her own jacket round Andi's shoulders. She shivered with cold and shock. Moonlight showed cuts and bruises on her hands and face. She sat forward, hugging her knees, waiting for the ambulance.

It came, with a police escort, lights blazing along the lakeside, sirens screaming. Figures leapt out of the cars and ran down the slope towards them. Mandy stood waving both arms, calling loudly. Dorian rolled his eyes and skittered at the dreadful noise.

Four men trampled the undergrowth. They brought a stretcher, medical bags, ropes, lights.

'Over here!' Mandy yelled.

They ran, out of control, down the steep slope.

Dorian reared up in fright. He hated the sirens and the shadowy, hurtling shapes. Two of the men scrambled to a standstill. They shoved the donkey to one side.

'Oh, watch out!' Andi cried.

Dorian missed his footing and slipped. He crashed back towards the water, down into the waterfall, scrambling at the wet rock-face, crashing and slipping out of sight.

'Mandy, find Dorian for me!' Andi pleaded as she was carried off.

As the medical team took expert care of Andi, Mandy ran to the waterfall. She felt the spray on her face, the water splashed over her hands as she knelt to look. She thought she saw Dorian, way below by the wooden bridge, limping painfully on three legs. But perhaps it was a shadow. She heard nothing except the roar of the water. She called his name.

Then her mother and father came scrambling down the slope with James. They flung a coat round her, told her she must hurry to the ambulance. She resisted. 'Where's Dorian?' she repeated over and over.

'Never mind now, love,' Mum whispered. 'Let's get you both to hospital.' She held her by the shoulder as they climbed to the road.

'James, you've got to find Dorian!' she gasped. But she was exhausted, confused, almost collapsing with the strain of the last half hour. 'He saved Andi's life!'

They all promised to do their best. The important thing was to get the girls to hospital. Tomorrow they'd look for the donkey. Andi was the person they had to worry about first.

Nine

Andi was kept in hospital overnight. Her left arm was broken above the elbow. Her cuts and bruises weren't serious, but the doctor warned her that she would be stiff and sore. He examined Mandy and then allowed her to go home. She and James looked in on Andi's ward just before midnight.

She sat up in bed, looking pale and serious. Stephen and Silvia Greenaway were at her side. She smiled at Mandy. 'Thanks. You two were brilliant.'

Mandy blushed. She didn't see that she and James had done anything out of the ordinary. 'Will you still be able to play tennis?' she asked.

Andi nodded. 'Yes. My right arm is the one that counts, thank goodness.'

'No need to think about that just yet,' Mr Greenaway said. He looked strained, but tried to put on a brave face. 'We just want you fit and well!'

Mandy stood at the end of the clean, white bed. She felt Andi was avoiding the only question she really wanted to ask. 'Listen, Andi . . . about Dorian,' she began.

'You didn't find him, did you?' Andi leaned forward, grasping the sheet.

'No, not yet. But we'll be out there looking as soon as it gets light. Don't worry.'

Andi sighed and looked down.

'He'll be OK, you'll see. You know Dorian!' Mandy felt he could take care of himself better than anyone.

'We'll go back to the waterfall and start looking,' James promised.

'Let me know as soon as you hear anything!'

Silvia leaned over and took her daughter's hand. 'Now it's time for Adam and Emily to take these two home, and for you to get some sleep,' she said gently.

Mrs Hope agreed to run Mandy and James over

to Tindle before surgery next morning. She smiled as she dropped them off on the road by the waterfall. 'I'll call in at some of the farms on the way back,' she promised. 'I'll ask people to keep a lookout for a donkey. I expect he's just rested overnight and is heading for home this very moment!' She smiled again, then drove off, having made Mandy promise to ring Animal Ark as soon as she had any news.

James and Mandy made their way down to the scene of the previous night's accident. In the dull light of an overcast sky, the crevice looked shadowy and dangerous. It was half-hidden by bushes and ferns; easy to see how Dorian had stumbled and thrown Andi off his back. The slope was steep and the ground scattered with loose rocks. Beyond the crevice the stream fell and splashed over big ledges, throwing up white spray. The banks were bright green with slippery moss.

'OK?' Mandy asked James. She prepared to descend, close to the water's edge.

He nodded. 'We should be getting good at this by now.'

Mandy bit her tongue. She had a secret fear; a picture of Dorian vanishing over the edge of the rock into the dark water. She remembered the silence after his fall.

'Let's check for hoof-prints!' James was eager to begin. He pushed aside small, overhanging branches, then seized a long, straight stick to beat back the bushes. He found he had to cling on to roots and find safe footholds on the steep slope down.

Mandy swallowed hard before she followed him. *I hope we don't find Dorian anywhere near here!* she said to herself. She dreaded finding him badly injured, or worse, at the foot of some sheer drop.

'Not here!' James reported as he reached the wooden footbridge at the bottom of the slope. He looked back up at Mandy. 'I suppose that's a relief in a way!'

She jumped down to join him and smiled. 'Great minds think alike! Come on!'

They began to scout around on level ground, looking for fresh signs. But they found only old prints of the donkey's hooves climbing up the slope with Andi on his back. There were none at all showing Dorian heading home.

'Where are you, Dorian?' James shouted out loud. He turned to Mandy. 'He can't just vanish!'

But they spent a long morning searching the

lakeside and the fields and farms to either side of the old bridle-path. No luck; Dorian was nowhere to be found.

'No, sorry,' the old farmers said one after another. 'That nice young woman vet called in earlier this morning, asking after the old chap. I told her I'd keep a sharp lookout.'

Mandy and James thanked them and ran on, quick as they could.

'I've got better things to do with my time than look out for a daft old donkey!' Dora Janeki snapped. She was a thin, bad-tempered woman who lived on a lonely farm next to the moorside. 'I've got shearing starting tomorrow, and fifty sheep to round up in the top fields!' She stamped off.

Mandy shrugged. Discouraged, she and James made their way back home.

'No luck?' Adam Hope met them in the doorway to the surgery. He was going down to Manor Farm to help the Greenaways pack. He told them that Silvia and Andi were coming to stay at Animal Ark for a few days, once Andi got out of hospital. 'She needs somewhere to rest and get over this business of the fall,' he explained. 'It's shaken her up pretty badly. And of course they have to be out of their house by tomorrow. So Mum thought it would help if Andi could stay close by, just until she's fit and well again.'

'Oh, good.' Mandy nodded. But she felt bitterly disappointed after their failed search. Nothing would give her a greater thrill than announcing to Andi that Dorian had turned up. But where was he? How could he disappear so completely and without trace?

'Cheer up. Have some lunch, then it won't feel so bad,' Dad said. He turned and went off whistling quietly down the lane.

They dragged themselves indoors. 'Don't worry, we'll try again this afternoon,' James promised. 'We'll keep on looking until we find him!'

'I'm glad I'm not in this by myself,' Mandy told him. James never let her down. He was always there. She couldn't wish for a better friend.

He blushed and shoved his hair back from his forehead. 'I'd better ring my mum and tell her not to expect me back home this afternoon,' he replied, practical as ever.

Three more days went by. Stephen Greenaway's new football team needed him to start work, so he left Mrs Greenaway to look after Andi. When

Andi came out of hospital, her arm in plaster, she and her mother went to stay with the Hopes at Animal Ark. Every spare moment, during those long midsummer days, Mandy and James would spend combing the hillsides, returning to Tindle, searching every square metre of ground. Each time they came home disappointed.

'We're not giving up!' Mandy promised the older girl one afternoon, as they sat in Mandy's cosy bedroom surrounded by the faces of beautiful, fluffy kittens, thoroughbred Arabians and friendly golden labradors. They all stared down from her glossy posters. 'We're going to find Dorian if it's the last thing we do!'

Andi smiled. She was still pale and weak from the accident. 'The thing is, I'm sure Dorian wouldn't just go missing that night. He'd get home if he possibly could!' Her voice sounded shaky and afraid. 'You know what he's like; he can't keep his nose out of anything! He's not happy unless he's got someone to talk to!' She sighed and gazed out of the window, down the hill towards the village. 'Oh, Mandy, where do you think he's gone? What's happened to him?'

Mandy could only shake her head. But that afternoon she cycled over to James's house to talk him into another search. She wanted to go in the direction of Walton, the large town down the dale where James and Mandy both went to school. They must think again, begin to look further afield.

James agreed. 'OK, it can't do any harm. Let's ask down in the village too.' They set off together.

'I should think everyone from here to York already knows we're looking for Dorian!' Mandy said as they rode along. 'Still, we can check if you like.'

But in the McFarlanes' post office and all down the main street, they met with the same answer; 'No, sorry, love. I haven't seen him. I'll keep my ears open, though, and let you know if I do!'

Mandy sighed. 'Let's try Jude and Rowan. They know everything that's going on round here. We're heading in the right direction, in any case.' They were cycling along the flat stretch of Walton Road. Somehow Mandy felt that the travelling family would help to cheer them up, whether or not they had news of Dorian.

But once more they were out of luck. They rang the doorbell at The Riddings, and stood admiring the work that Jude had done to the garden. Perfect pink roses bloomed on neat bushes, the lawn looked smooth as a bowling green.

The door burst open. 'Come in, come in!' Marjorie Spry beamed at them as she ushered them into the hall.

The heaped piles of yellow newspapers were gone, shelves and windowsills were shiny and clean. Even the floor sparkled, and everywhere there was a smell of lavender polish.

'Wow!' James couldn't disguise his surprise. Last time he'd seen inside this place, there was dust and cobwebs everywhere.

'All thanks to Mrs Somers!' Miss Marjorie said proudly. 'Joan pretends not to like it, but I know better!'

'Is Rowan around? We'd like to speak to her, please.' Mandy thought she'd better come to the point. 'We're looking for that donkey again.'

'The one out in our conservatory?' Miss Marjorie's eyes widened.

'What, now?' For a second Mandy's heart leapt. The Spry twins were eccentric enough to be keeping Dorian quietly hidden in their conservatory.

'No, dear. Last week, wasn't it? You know!' Miss Marjorie put her bird-like head to one side and sighed. 'In any case, you're too late to speak to Mrs Somers, I'm afraid.'

'Too late?' James looked round the spruce house, through all the open doors. 'Do you mean that Jude and Rowan have gone?'

'They left us!' Miss Joan cackled from the library. She'd been eavesdropping. Now she sailed into view, head up, cradling Patch in one arm. 'Gone! Left us in peace at last!'

'Oh!' Disappointed, Mandy began to back out of the door. 'Sorry to bother you. We didn't realise.' Joan Spry must have been too much even for easy-going Jude and his family to put up with.

'No, no, dear, it's not like that!' Miss Marjorie seized her arm and dragged her back inside. 'We like them very much!'

'We don't!' Miss Joan contradicted.

'We do! Now, Joan, be quiet.' Miss Marjorie silenced her sister. 'What's more, and much to my surprise, *they* like us!'

'That's great!' James looked relieved. 'Where are they now, then?'

'We came to an arrangement. They've agreed to come to work for us for two days every week. But they said they missed the open road, and I must confess I don't blame them! All that fresh air! All that freedom!' Miss Marjorie glared at her twin sister. 'Freedom to go where one chooses!'

'So they go off for a few days, then come back here?' Mandy thought she understood.

'Yes, dear. At least for the summer. Whatever Mrs Ponsonby and Mrs Platt may have to say about it!' She flashed them a mischievous smile. 'That way we manage to keep our house and garden in good order, and they receive a wage from us. For the rest of the time they can come and go as they please. It's perfect!'

Mandy and James smiled happily. It was odd, but true. The Spry sisters and the Somers family were made for one another.

'And if you hurry up and chase after them,' Miss Joan said with a spiteful glance, 'you'll be able to catch up with them!'

'Why, which way did they go?' James asked.

Miss Joan sniffed. 'Up towards the Beacon.' She pointed airily to the Celtic cross on the moorside. 'Just before lunch. Shoo! Go along, hurry!' She waved them out of the house.

James and Mandy grinned at one another again as they grabbed their bikes and cycled off. They sped back through the village and up on to the moor road. The red van would be easy to spot. Mandy looked forward to meeting up with their friends. 'At least we can ask them to keep an eye

open for Dorian,' she said. She liked to feel the
wind in her hair, and the swoop of her bike as
they dropped into a dip on the narrow, lonely
road.

'Up there, look!' James pointed to the lookout
spot at the crest of the next hill. Sure enough, the
battered red van came into view, parked on the
wide gravel area just along from the bridle-path.
'It looks pretty deserted though.' The doors were
all shut up and there was no one around. Mandy
and James pedalled hard uphill. 'Maybe they all
went for a walk.'

Mandy came round a bend and jammed on her
brakes. James swerved and skidded behind her.
'Watch out!' he yelled.

'Look!' she cried.

There was a procession coming down the road
towards them. It walked into the sunshine out of
the shade of a high, heathery bank. Jude Somers
strode along at the head, with little Jason riding
high on his shoulders. The boy waved his arms
and sang. Rowan walked behind, holding Skye's
hand. The little girl wore a bright lemon and pink
T-shirt. Her legs were brown. The two lean dogs,
Joey and Spider, ranged along the grass verge with
their long, loping strides, sniffing out rabbits. And

behind them, held on a loose rope, limping slightly on his left foreleg, but head up and going at a smart pace, was someone they couldn't fail to recognise.

He spotted them standing open-mouthed on the roadside. *About time too!* his bossy nod of the head suggested. *What on earth kept you?*

'Dorian!' Mandy and James shouted together. 'Where have you been?'

They ditched their bikes and ran to meet him. The children squealed with delight. Mandy flung her arms round Dorian's neck and buried her face in his soft brown coat.

James grinned at Jude. 'Where did you find him?'

'We didn't. He found us.' Jude wore a broad smile. 'We thought we'd see him on his way and help him home. You can see he's limping a bit.'

'Oh, Dorian, what happened? Oh, I'm so glad to see you!' Mandy hugged and hugged him. She was beside herself with happiness. 'We were afraid you were dead!'

Dorian nudged her away to arm's length and gave her a sideways looks. *Don't make a fuss!*

It was true that he was a little the worse for wear – dusty and much thinner – but it would take more than a little fall down a wet rock to finish him off. *Now let's get on, shall we?* he suggested with an impatient toss of his head.

'Here!' Rowan laughed handing Mandy the halter rope. 'He's all yours!'

Mandy felt as though she would burst with joy as Dorian took charge and limped ahead. He was in a hurry to get home at last.

Ten

Dorian limped through Welford at the head of the colourful procession of children, grown-ups, dogs and bikes. It was teatime. Ernie Bell and Walter Pickard gave them a wave and a smile from their garden gates. 'Well done. We knew you'd sort it out in the end!' they called.

Mrs Ponsonby teetered on the step outside the McFarlanes' post office. She scooped precious Pandora up into her arms and tutted loudly at the sight of the Somers family.

But Joey and Spider went over and wagged their long, thin tails at Toby. The mongrel wagged his in return. 'Oh . . . oh well, Pandora, I suppose you'd better say hello too!' Gingerly Mrs Ponsonby put the dog down. The Pekinese gave Joey and Spider a gracious welcome. 'Nice doggies!' Mrs Ponsonby proclaimed. She gave Mandy a royal wave.

Mandy smiled back and followed close on Dorian's heels. He turned swiftly into their lane and gathered speed, in spite of his limp.

Rowan laughed. 'He's in charge!' They almost had to run to keep up.

Animal Ark was in sight. 'As usual!' Mandy gasped. 'The trouble is, I'm sure he thinks he's going home!'

James threw his bike down on to the grass verge. 'Hadn't we better try to stop him?'

'Yes, there's a terrible shock in store for him at Manor Farm.'

'Have the new people moved in yet?'

Mandy nodded. 'As soon as the Greenaways moved out. We saw the furniture van go down the lane two or three days ago. We don't even know who the new owners are yet. One thing is for sure; Dorian's in for a big disappointment when he finally arrives!'

'Whoa, boy!' James ran ahead and tried to rein the donkey back so they could explain.

But Dorian had got it into his head that he was going home. He strained at the rein and forged ahead, straight past Animal Ark, heading for Lilac Cottage.

'Who said donkeys weren't stubborn?' James complained. His arms felt as if they were being pulled out of their sockets as Dorian dragged him along.

Mandy ran alongside. 'He's not stubborn. He just knows his own mind, that's all.'

Skye and Jason trotted and skipped to keep up. They clapped their hands and laughed. Jude and Rowan strode along to keep them company. 'This is something I just *have* to see!' Jude said with a grin.

'Hang on, I'd better go and warn Andi!' James said. He was red in the face from the effort of trying to control Dorian. 'She'll have to come and explain!' Quickly he slipped back up the drive to Animal Ark.

But Dorian gathered speed. He trotted past the neat hedges of Lilac Cottage, at the head of the procession. They sped on, past the small common where the Somers had once parked, down the narrow, twisting lane to Manor Farm.

'Listen, Dorian!' Mandy said, out of breath and

growing more alarmed. 'Andi doesn't live there any more! She's at our house!'

But Dorian took no notice. His head was up, his ears forward. The end was in sight.

'Oh dear!' Mandy hesitated at the gate as Dorian broke free and nipped down the long drive to Manor Farm. A glance to the rear showed her that James was catching them up with Andi, who half-laughed, half-cried as she stumbled along with her arm in its sling. Ahead, Dorian broke into a canter. He'd spotted his old paddock. His stable door stood half-open.

'Come on!' Jude insisted. 'We'd better follow him and see what we can do to help.' The procession straggled down the drive.

Dorian cantered on into the stable yard. His enormous bray echoed through the valley. *I'm back!* The new family came running out of the house. Mandy saw a boy of about ten, then a man and a woman, all standing open-mouthed in the stable yard.

Dorian stared at them with a frown. He pawed the yard. He glanced towards the stable, then trotted forward. He began to nudge the nervous looking woman to one side. He peered through the doorway into the house.

'Oh no!' Mandy groaned. 'They're going to chuck him out!' They'd arrived at the farm too late.

'No, just watch this!' Rowan pointed. She put out a hand to stop James and Andi from overtaking them and leaping in to restrain the donkey. 'I'm sure Dorian can handle this!'

Dorian backed a little way out of the doorway. He looked down his nose at the new family.

'Don't worry, I'll take care of this!' The angry father, a stout, grey-haired man still dressed in the suit he'd worn to work that day, began to stride towards Mandy's motley group.

'Oh, Mum!' the fair-haired boy protested. He approached Dorian, head on one side.

'Jack, keep away! He could turn nasty!' The mother stared anxiously at Dorian.

Dorian lowered his large head and nuzzled the boy's side. He nosed into his pockets.

'He winked! Did you see that? Dorian just winked at us!' Mandy was certain it was true.

'Shh!' Andi held her breath. 'I think he's decided that he likes them!'

'He's just being friendly, that's all. Mum, have we got a carrot?' Jack laughed at the feel of Dorian's soft nose. The woman disappeared into the house and returned holding a large carrot. 'Hold it in the flat of your hand, Mum. That's right. He won't hurt you. He's a soft old thing. There, see!' Dorian snaffled the carrot. He crunched it with evident relish, showing them his big front teeth.

'Well!' Jack's mother declared. 'He certainly knows how to get what he wants!' She stood, a smile hovering on her lips. Then she stretched out a nervous hand to say hello.

'Whose donkey is this?' the father demanded. His anger was beginning to fade, but he looked confused.

Andi stepped forward. "Hello. I'm afraid he's mine. Well, he *was* mine but now we have to find him a new home.' She choked over the words.

'You're the girl who's just moved out of here, aren't you?' The man's face lit up with recognition. 'You're Andi Greenaway, the young tennis player! My, it looks as if you've been in the wars!' He looked at her injured arm, her cuts and bruises. Then he frowned and scratched his cheek, looking round at Dorian. 'I suppose he thinks you still live here . . .'

Mandy and James stood waiting in the stable yard as everything slotted into place for the new owners of Manor Farm. Dorian glanced round at them from his position in the doorway. He bared his teeth in a smile. Jack meanwhile had flung his arms round the donkey's neck. 'Mum, we can keep him, can't we? This is his home, after all! He's come back and we can't just send him away again!'

Mandy grasped Andi by the hand. 'The cunning old thing! I bet Dorian knew what he was doing all along!'

But Jack's mum looked doubtful. 'Oh, I don't know, dear. We've already taken on an awful lot!'

Mandy couldn't bear to hear any more. 'At least he's safe!' she breathed to Andi. 'Though goodness knows where he's been these past few days!'

'I know!' Andi gabbled out an explanation about a phone call they'd had at Animal Ark just a few minutes before Dorian had led the procession down the lane. 'It was Dora Janeki. She told us she'd just had to chase an old donkey from her hay barn up on the hill. He must have been there for days, she said, and she didn't sound too pleased about it!'

'Uh-oh!' James laughed. 'Dorian would have to choose *her* barn, wouldn't he? The only person who refused to help us look in the first place!'

Andi nodded. 'Well, Mr Hope reckoned he'd

probably got as far as he could that night on his injured leg. Then he realised he would have to rest until the sprain healed. Donkeys always know when they've reached their limit. It just so happened it was Mrs Janeki's barn. And lucky in one way, because there was hay for him to eat. But then today she went in to stack some wool from shearing, and came face to face with Dorian! Like I say, she wasn't too pleased. She sent him packing.'

'Poor Dorian!' Mandy grinned. He'd met his match with Dora Janeki. She gazed across to where he stood, ears twitching, keen to join in the conversation about his future.

' . . . Only one little donkey!' Jack pleaded.

Dorian sniggered and nodded.

'Little!' His father's eyebrows shot up as he stared Dorian in the eye. 'How much hay do you think he gets through in one week? Who's going to pay for it?'

'But we can't throw him out! He's got nowhere to go!' Jack pointed out in a high, strained voice. 'This is his home!'

Dorian sighed.

The waiting was agony for Mandy. 'At least he's safe!' she repeated. 'But wouldn't it be wonderful if Dorian got his own way at last?'

As if there's any doubt! he suggested with a knowing glance.

'Oh, all right!' Jack's mum said at last. 'I suppose he is rather sweet.'

Dorian jerked his head and snorted.

'Can he stay?' Jack insisted.

'Yes, he can stay at Manor Farm!' his father said.

Andi ran forward with a delighted cry. Mandy had to stop herself from running forward too. She stayed with James and the Somers family. Dorian gently broke free from his new owners and trotted to greet Andi. *No need to worry your head about me,*

he said with a little bob of his head.

Andi's face was wreathed in smiles as she hugged him and rested her cheek against his neck.

'Now she's happy, she can go off and play tennis,' James said. 'And be a champion.'

'She can come back and visit Dorian whenever she wants!' Mandy added.

The donkey stepped forward to rattle the stable door. He knew it was time to rest. He looked round at them, paused on the doorstep of his old home. He took a nip of hay from his old haynet, and sighed as he wandered in, home at last!

Mandy grinned. 'Trust Dorian!' she said. 'He must have been born under a lucky star!'

The donkey turned and looked her straight in the eye. *Luck has nothing to do with it!* he said with a wink. And Mandy suspected that he'd planned every move!